He just wanted to get to know the obstinate woman...

"I'm a pretty good listener, Jess. And anything you tell me would be strictly confidential. You have my word."

She looked up at him with those big blue eyes, and the temptation to pull her into his arms nearly overpowered him. Their earlier kiss had been cut short, and he hadn't been able to think about much since.

"There's nothing to tell," she insisted. "I got married too young, and he turned out to be a total loser. End of story."

Having hoped she would open up to him, Garrett felt a surprising sense of disappointment. "Fine. If that's the way you want it, I won't push." He swiped his fingers through his hair. "Your business is your business."

"Finally," she said with a playful roll of her eyes. "Listen, it's been great fun and all, but I have to get up early for work. So, if you wouldn't mind..." She gestured toward the door.

Garrett shook his head and chuckled. "Woman, you are hell on a man's ego."

"Somehow, I think you'll live."

"Well?" He stood up and motioned her forward. "Aren't you going to send me off with a good night kiss?"

She let out a delicate snort. "You act as if we're dating or something. Hell, we just got past our mutual dislike of each other."

"Is 'mutual dislike' what you were feeling when you wrapped your arms and legs around me in the kitchen?" he asked, annoyed by her casual attitude. "Because it's definitely not what I was feeling."

REVIEWS FOR DONNA MARIE ROGERS

There's Only Been You

"Love lost and found is the basis of this wonderfully heartwarming read. Throw in a years-old lie and a strong sense of family and it only gets better and better."
—4 Stars, RT Book Reviews

"Donna Marie Rogers delivers a tender tale of love, family, and second chances."
—5 Bookmarks, Wild on Books

Meant To Be

"The plot kept me spellbound throughout the entire book. Rogers has the ability to keep her readers on the edge of our seats."
—5 Hearts, The Romance Studio

"The material is tightly written, well plotted and fast paced, and the characters are unforgettable."
—5 Books, Long and Short Reviews

Welcome To Redemption Series

"With their easy, breezy style and skilled characterizations, Rogers and Netzel have created a town that readers won't want to leave."
—4½ Stars - RT Book Reviews

OTHER TITLES

Jamison Series

There's Only Been You, Book 1
Foolish Pride (Extra Peek Short Story)
Meant To Be, Book 2

Golden Series
(Contemporary Western Romance)

Golden Opportunity, Book 1

Welcome To Redemption Series
(with Stacey Joy Netzel)

A Fair of the Heart, Book 1, Donna Marie Rogers
A Fair to Remember, Book 2, Stacey Joy Netzel
The Perfect Blend, Book 3, Donna Marie Rogers
Grounds For Change, Book 4, Stacey Joy Netzel
Home Is Where the Heart Is, Book 5, Donna Marie Rogers
The Heart of the Matter, Book 6, Stacey Joy Netzel
Never Let Me Go, Book 7, Donna Marie Rogers
Hold On To Me, Book 8, Stacey Joy Netzel

Writing as Liza James:
Only Man For the Job
Mischief in the Dark
Branded
Game On
Lying Eyes
Hot For Teacher

Dedication

To my NovelFriends—Stacey, Jamie and Dulcie. If not for you and our GNOs, I'd be a raving lunatic. Thanks for keeping me grounded…and sane.
Love you guys.

Also, to the best 'moms' a girl could have—
Virginia & Mary Jo.
You both mean the world to me.

This is a work of fiction. Names, characters, places, and incidents are either the product of the author's imagination or are used fictitiously, and any resemblance to actual persons living or dead, business establishments, events, or locales, is entirely coincidental.

Copyright © 2013 Author Edition
Meant To Be by Donna Marie Rogers
First Published 2008 by The Wild Rose Press

All Rights Reserved. No part of this book may be used or reproduced in any manner whatsoever without written permission of the author except in the case of brief quotations embodied in critical articles or reviews.

Edited by Stacy D. Holmes
Cover art by The Killion Group
Formatted by Author E.M.S.

ISBN-13: 978-1490482897
ISBN-10: 149048289X

Meant To Be

DONNA MARIE ROGERS

One

Garrett Jamison stormed out of the car dealership, his aggravation level at an all-time high. *Idiots*. How hard was it to change the oil, spark plugs, and slap on a couple of new tires? Christ, he could've done a faster job with a can opener and a hammer.

With an hour yet to kill before his truck was ready, Garrett weaved his way across six lanes of traffic and headed for the restaurant on the corner. *Please let them make a decent cup of coffee.* He shoved the door open with more force than necessary, stalked past the sign that read PLEASE WAIT TO BE SEATED, and slid into a dark green booth in the farthest corner of the room.

He glanced around with little interest. Typical family-style restaurant. Quaint yet forgettable paintings of waterfalls and landscapes graced each wall. A fake potted ivy hung from the ceiling above and to the left of him, directly over a stack of green and brown plastic booster seats and trayless wooden highchairs. The tempting aromas of everything from bacon and smoked ham to fresh blueberry muffins and syrup-dripping pancakes made his mouth water and his stomach grumble.

A good five minutes went by, and still no waitress.

Jesus, what does a guy have to do to get a cup of coffee in this place? He flipped his cup over and dumped in a couple of creamers.

Elbow resting on the table, face cradled in his open hand, Garrett skimmed one of the pamphlets he'd grabbed from the dealership. He was on the verge of storming out when he heard soft footsteps approach.

"'Bout time." He folded up the pamphlet and rubbed his eyes. "I'll take a cup of coffee and a slice of apple pie with..." His words trailed off when he glanced up and got a look at his waitress. "You've *got* to be kidding me."

Garrett hadn't had a decent night's sleep in days thanks to his irritating new neighbor standing before him—and her howling cat. She and the mammoth fur ball had moved in a couple of weeks ago, and if they stayed much longer, he'd be lucky to keep his sanity.

"Yeah, I'm getting that warm, fuzzy feeling myself," Jessica McGovern muttered, pen poised over her order tablet. "So, what do you want with your pie?"

"A new waitress."

Her eyes narrowed. "You just can't help being a jerk, can you? How you could possibly be related to the rest of your family is beyond me."

"Well, you can thank that squealing tub of lard you call a cat for my cheery disposition. Which reminds me, have you had that thing euthanized yet? 'Cause I could probably get you a discount at the animal hospital down the road."

"You're disgusting," she shot back. "No wonder you're not married. What woman would have you?"

He leaned back and draped his arm across the back of the booth. "Well, I don't see a ring on your finger either, *sweetheart*."

"I'm divorced, not that it's any of your business."

He smirked. "Now, there's a surprise. What's amazing is he actually went through with the ceremony. And please don't tell me you have kids, because any spawn of yours would be—"

Jessica hauled off and slapped him so hard Garrett was shocked into stunned silence. The sound was so loud it reverberated across the room, silencing the majority of patrons and restaurant staff.

Garrett had a feeling if he glanced in a mirror, he'd be able to watch the imprint of her hand materialize on his cheek like a Polaroid picture. And damn if it didn't sting like hell.

She gaped at him, eyes widened in horror. But some raw emotion had darkened those eyes just before she struck him. He suddenly felt like a first-class jackass for causing her such pain. What the hell was the matter with him?

Jessica's manager, a short, middle-aged man with a receding hairline and scar slashed across the corner of his mouth making it look as if he had a perpetual pout, came barreling forward, his dour expression not boding well for her.

"Mr. Turner, I can explain, I—"

He shot Jessica a quick scowl before turning to face Garrett. "Sir, I would like to offer a most sincere apology, and of course, your meal's on the house."

He turned back to confront Jessica. "Ms. McGovern, needless to say, you're *fired*. Please collect your purse and punch out. I'll be back there in a few minutes to cut you a check."

Before she could respond, Garrett rose to his full height and towered over the squat little man. "I'm afraid what just happened was entirely my fault. I'm ashamed to admit I made a rather vulgar comment, and the lady here merely reacted as any decent woman would. I guess you could say I got what I deserved."

Garrett glanced down at Jessica, who cocked a brow, but remained silent.

"Sir, that may be, but I can't have someone in my employ who would strike a customer, regardless of the reason."

"Listen, what if she offers me an apology and promises never to do it again?"

"I don't know." Mr. Turner seemed less than thrilled with the idea. He did a quick scan of the restaurant as if seeking approval from the other customers.

"Come on, Ms. McGovern," Garrett coaxed. "Say you're sorry so I can get that pie and coffee I came in here for, and you can get back to work. I'm sure the rest of your customers are just as hungry as I am." He held her gaze, daring her to argue.

She clenched her hands, no doubt itching to smack him again. "I'm terribly sorry for slapping you across the face."

"I accept your apology. Mr. Turner, I hope this settles it. And since I do feel responsible for what happened, I insist on paying my own check."

The manager glanced back and forth between them before giving a curt nod. "All right then. Ms. McGovern, I suggest you get back to work." He turned back to Garrett. "Mr., uh—?"

"Jamison. Officer Garrett Jamison."

Mr. Turner gave an owlish blink and cleared his throat. "Officer Jamison, again, I apologize." He turned on his heel and marched away.

Garrett sat back down as Jessica followed after her boss. She cast Garrett an odd glance over her shoulder before disappearing into the kitchen.

Well, he had to admit, she had his attention. She'd given as good as she got until he'd made that thoughtless comment about her having kids. Garrett's face prickled with shame. He knew how he'd feel if someone made a similar comment to his sister, Sara.

Jessica reappeared from the kitchen. Viewing her suddenly in a new light, he watched her approach with his pie and a pot of coffee. She was tiny like Sara, maybe five-foot-two, but there was something regal about the way she walked that made her seem more imposing. Her body was perfection, too, with curves in all the right places. And if he hadn't been wallowing in self-pity for the past couple of weeks, maybe he'd have noticed sooner.

"You never did say what you wanted with your pie." She set his plate down and filled his cup with the steaming brew. "So I topped it with whipped cream."

How could he not have realized how gorgeous those big blue eyes were before? Maybe they just seemed more pronounced with her honey-blonde hair pulled back into a fat bun. When free, he knew it flowed well past her shoulders in thick waves—

Fingers snapped in front of his nose.

"Look toward the light, Jamison," she intoned. "Follow the sound of my voice."

He grinned. She had a good sense of humor, too, which, let's face it, a woman would have to have to put up with his moody ass. "Whipped cream is fine."

She crossed her arms. "But it isn't what you wanted, right?"

"I would've preferred a la mode, but I like whipped cream as well."

Her eyes narrowed. "Hey, what's up with the personality change?"

"What are you talking about?" He held his palms up in mock supplication. "I'm always a happy-go-lucky guy."

She let out an unladylike snort. "Yeah, and I'm Sofia Vergara. No, seriously, why the turnaround? I slapped you across the face, and it was like flipping a switch from monster to human being."

"Careful," he drawled, "you might make me blush with such sweet words." He noticed someone gesturing for her. "Go take care of the rest of your customers, and let me eat my pie in peace, will you?"

She rolled her eyes. "Whatever."

Mesmerized by the sway of her hips as she walked away, Garrett decided he may have been a bit too hasty in his first impression.

At the end of her shift, Jessica snatched her purse out of her locker and clocked out. *Big idiot cop.* Okay, so he'd saved her from getting fired. *Big whoopty-do.* Her job wouldn't have been in jeopardy in the first place if he hadn't provoked her to violence.

Come on, Jessie, we're all responsible for our own actions.

Oh, shut up.

After a ten minute ride, Jessica pulled her old pickup into the driveway and killed the engine. She eyeballed Garrett Jamison's truck, tempted to sneak over and let the air out of his tires. *Nope*, she thought with a wistful twist of her lips. *Not worth a night in jail.*

She grabbed her purse and the beef melt sandwich she'd brought home for supper, and headed into the house.

Once settled in her old rocker-recliner with her sandwich and a bottle of iced-tea, she clicked on the TV. The five o'clock news would be on soon, and she leaned back in the comfortable beige chair, plate balanced on her lap, curious to know more about her new hometown of Green Bay, Wisconsin.

Hard to believe she'd only been here a couple of weeks. Seemed more like months had gone by since she'd packed up her truck and traveled halfway across the country. She'd rented the house in advance from her Great Uncle Charlie and had been lucky enough to find full-time employment on her fourth night in town. The minimum wage job would barely cover all her bills, however, so she'd need to find something part-time before she ended up dipping into the little bit of savings she had.

She tilted the bottle to her lips and took a sip of her tea. So far, she loved it here. The city itself was beautiful, particularly the rural neighborhood Uncle Charlie lived in. White flowering trees lined both sides of the street, and just about everybody had a basketful of petunias, begonias, or some such flower hanging by their front door. The people were just as friendly as she'd always heard Midwesterners were, too.

With the exception of the Jolly Mean Giant next door.

And what a waste since the man was as gorgeous as they came. Thick, near-black hair curled up around the nape of his neck; dark, bedroom brown eyes framed by thick lashes any woman would envy. Not to mention, the sexiest dimples she'd ever seen—which she'd only seen once, when he'd smiled down at his sister's kid. The guy was huge, too, well over six feet tall and solidly built, with muscular arms that just bordered on being too thick. The kind of arms a girl could feel safe in.

Disgusted by the direction of her thoughts, she unwrapped her sandwich and sank her teeth in. Maybe some major chewing would get the big jerk out of her mind.

Mr. Louie hopped up on her lap, stuck his little pink nose into the melted cheese, and let out a whopper of a sneeze.

"Oh, gross! Thanks a lot, cat."

Mr. Louie grinned up at her. She eyed the sandwich with regret before setting the plate on the floor. *Taps* bugled in her mind as she watched the little crapper devour her supper.

Having pretty much lost her appetite, and her desire to watch the news, Jessica got up and headed into the bedroom. Might as well fire up her laptop and see if her online service was in a more accommodating mood than it'd been yesterday.

Garrett was lifting weights in the basement when he heard the front door fly open and the familiar tread of small feet race across the floor above him.

"Uncle Garrett! Uncle Garrett! I mastered it! I mastered Combat Commando!"

Grinning, Garrett listened to the staccato clip of those feet as they flew through the kitchen, down the basement steps, until his nephew, Ethan, skidded to a halt in front of him.

"Mastered it? Holy cow, sport. That's amazing." He set the barbell down and reached for a towel. "Maybe we can play a few rounds later tonight, if it's okay with your parents."

"Sounds good to this parent," Mike Andrews assured him as he descended the stairs and strode over to stand beside his son.

It never failed to amaze Garrett just how much father and son resembled each other, with their nearly black hair and unnaturally bright blue eyes. "Hey, Mike."

"Garrett." He reached out and shook his hand. "Ethan was hoping he could spend the night here, if you don't have plans. Please say you don't have plans."

Garrett grinned. "You and Sara not getting much *alone time*?"

"Not as much as I'd like, though I'm not complaining." Mike took a seat on the couch, legs sprawled and arms draped across the top. "Listen, there's something I'd like to talk to you about, if you've got a minute."

He glanced over at Ethan. "Hey, sport, why don't you get the game set up while I talk to your dad for a minute."

"Okay."

Garrett worked the towel down his neck and chest. "So, what's up?"

"Detective Brady put in for a transfer today. His wife got some big promotion, so they're moving down to Milwaukee."

"No kidding, hey?" Garrett laid the towel over his shoulder. "Can't say I envy him. Milwaukee? No goddamn thanks."

Mike chuckled. "I hear you. What I'm wondering is, you interested in making detective?"

Garrett let out a long-suffering breath. *Detective?* Hell, he'd been dreaming of making detective since the day he joined the police academy. Now he wasn't even sure he wanted to remain on the force, let alone move up the ranks. The most important asset a cop had was his instincts. He discovered his were worthless the night he got shot, and Ethan was kidnapped right out of his own bed—by Garrett's own partner.

"I'm not sure what I want to do anymore." He lowered his voice. "I've been thinking about taking a leave from the force. And that information stays between us, got it?"

Mike glanced at Ethan and it was almost as if understanding dawned. Garrett felt a stab of jealousy. It seemed that Mike's instincts were sharp as a tack.

"You're a good cop. Don't you think you're being a bit hard on yourself?"

Garrett shot to his feet and tossed the towel over the back of the weight bench. "There isn't anyone in this world I care about more than that boy," he said in a furious whisper. "And because of me, he almost died. Hard on myself? I should've had my badge stripped away, and you know it."

"Hey, Uncle Garrett, can I sleep over tonight? We can order pizza and play Combat Commando all night. I'll pay for the pizza. I got my allowance today." Ethan stuffed his hand in his front pocket and proudly pulled out a crumpled ten-dollar bill.

"That's mighty generous, Ethan, but I'll pay for the pizza. You just put your money in your piggy bank."

Ethan rolled his eyes. "It's a *Spiderman* bank."

He held up his hands. "Sorry."

Mike gave him one last, searching look before rising to his feet. "I have to get back home and fire up the grill. You sure it's all right if he sleeps over?"

The look on Mike's face was so hopeful, Garrett couldn't help but laugh. "I'm sure. I planned on staying in tonight anyway." He looked at Ethan. "It'll be a 'guys only' night. Pizza, root beer, chocolate cake, and Combat Commando. Uncle Luke and Uncle Nicky'll probably join us."

"Yay! I love whippin' Uncle Nicky at Combat Commando. He gets really mad and his eye starts twitchin'."

Garrett ruffled his hair. "Sounds good to me. You start practicing while I walk your dad out."

Mike gave Ethan a quick hug, then led the way upstairs.

"Hey, thanks again for taking Ethan." With a wink, Mike opened the front door.

Jessica raised her fist to knock at the exact moment the Jamison's front door swung open. Sara's fiancé, Mike—who was almost as large as Garrett—stepped out and nearly mowed her down. He caught himself in the nick of time.

"Whoa!"

She threw a hand up with a nervous laugh. "You just scared ten years off my life."

"Sorry." He shot her a sheepish grin. "Guess I'd better watch were I'm going. Garrett, thanks again. I'll talk to you later."

Jessica watched him leave before turning back to face Mr. Annoying. Standing there in nothing but a pair of black gym shorts, he was too hot for words. *Damn him.*

"So, what can I do for you?" He leaned negligently against the doorframe, a suspiciously pleasant smile curving his lips.

"I'm here to see Nick. Is he home?"

The smile disappeared. He straightened and crossed his arms over his chest, which made those huge biceps bulge even more. Jessica realized for the first time he had a tattoo. *Huh.* She wouldn't have taken him for the type. Frankly, she thought tattoos were sexy, if they weren't garish, which his wasn't. It looked to be some sort of Chinese symbols.

Probably means 'He-with-head-too-big-for-hat.'

"You're barking up the wrong tree there, honey. Nicky's married to his computer."

"Not that it's any of your business, but that's exactly why I'm here. I'm having trouble with a new program and was hoping he could help." Now why did she feel the urge to explain herself? *Double damn him.*

He raked her up and down in an insultingly blatant manner. "I know a thing or two about computers."

"No kidding? Great, next time I need help surfing the porno sites, you'll be the first one I call."

His eyes went cold. "You think I'm just some big, dumb Neanderthal, don't you?"

Jessica gave him the same insulting once over he'd given her. "If the leopard toga fits..."

"I happen to have a BS in Computer Science."

Hands on hips, jaw working furiously, he looked so offended Jessica was hard-pressed not to laugh. "Then

I'm stumped. You could be making a lot more money in computers than you are as a cop. And you wouldn't be putting your life in danger on a daily basis." She glanced meaningfully at the scarred flesh visible just above the waistband of his shorts, which she'd heard from his sister, Sara, was a gunshot wound.

"This didn't happen in the line of duty. Besides, I love being a cop."

He said it with such conviction; as if she should've instinctually *known* it. Jessica sighed. Garrett Jamison was turning out to be much deeper than she'd imagined. "It's a noble profession. It's also a very dangerous one."

"True enough. But it's not as if I have a family who's dependent on me."

She reached up to tuck a stray lock of hair behind her ear. "What about your uncle, or your sister and brothers? Or your nephew? I'm sure they'd all be devastated if something happened to you."

"What about you?"

His voice had taken on a deep, sexy timbre that turned Jessica's knees to mush. Garrett Jamison was entirely too gorgeous for his own good—or for hers.

"Wh-what about me?"

Before she knew it, he reached out and cupped the side of her face, tracing his thumb over her cheekbone. "Would you miss me if something happened?"

"What a thing to ask," she breathed, her gaze centered on his full lips. "I barely know you." Was he going to kiss her? Right there where any of the neighbors could see? Not that she'd mind...

"Uncle Garrett, the game's set up. Can we order pizza now?"

Garrett snatched back his hand, and Jessica's gaze

dropped to the little boy leaning possessively against his leg.

Was it her imagination, or was the little stinker glaring daggers at her?

"Hi, Ethan, my name is Jessica."

"I know."

Nope, not my imagination. In fact, the scowl the kid sported was downright hostile. Now what in the world had she done to deserve such disfavor?

"Ethan, you watch your manners," Garrett growled.

"Yes, sir."

He cast her one last, mutinous scowl, then turned and ran back into the house. Jessica resisted the urge to laugh. She wouldn't take his behavior personally. The boy obviously adored his uncle and didn't care to share him. Another fascinating layer of Garrett Jamison—loving uncle.

"Sorry about that. Ethan's a good kid. I'm not sure what got into him."

"My guess would be old-fashioned jealousy. You two apparently have plans for the evening, and when he saw us...talking, his young mind assumed I was trying to lure you away."

A frown creased his forehead. "I don't know. Ethan knows I'd never abandon him. For anyone."

Ouch, point taken. She shrugged. "You know him better than I do. I'm just telling you what I saw." She tucked her hair behind her ear and took a slight step back. "Well, this has been fun, but I need to get back. Mr. Louie doesn't like to watch TV alone."

Garrett chuckled. "Give His Highness a scratch behind the ears for me."

"What? Just this afternoon you suggested I have him

put down."

"Good Lord, woman, can't you take a joke?" Garrett winked at her, then stepped back and closed the door.

Jessica shook her head. The man was crazy, no doubt about it.

And so hot it should be a crime. *I'm too sex-y for my shirt, too sex-y for my shirt...*

Great, now she was losing it. Maybe she should make a citizen's arrest—for being a hazard to the sanity of women everywhere.

With a sigh of frustration, she headed back home to watch *Wheel of Fortune* with her cat. Nothing pathetic about that at all.

"She smacked you across the face in front of the entire restaurant?" Danny, Garrett's youngest brother, chuckled as he poured himself a cup of coffee. "Oh, man, I can only imagine what you must've said to piss her off that bad."

They'd just finished supper, and Ethan had wasted no time dragging Nicky downstairs to play video games when the subject turned to Jessica. Garrett had to wonder if maybe she'd been right about the jealousy thing.

"Son, I thought I taught you better," his uncle admonished, frowning. "You wouldn't want someone speaking to Sara like that, would you?"

Garrett took a thoughtful sip of his coffee. Uncle Luke had been thirty and single when he'd come to live with them after their parents were killed in a car crash nearly twenty years ago. He'd given up his freedom and any chance of having a life of his own with four young kids to raise, so there wasn't anyone in the world Garrett respected more. Or who knew him better.

"I've been in a funk lately, I know it. Believe me, I don't like it any better than the rest of you. Besides, I made sure she didn't lose her job. Doesn't that count for something?"

"You need to get laid, that's the problem," opined Danny.

"As if I need you to remind me of that." His brother happened to be the only man in the Jamison household with a sex life. He and his girlfriend, Emily, had gotten engaged a few weeks back, and Danny had unofficially moved in with her that same night.

Uncle Luke cleared his throat. "Garrett, do you happen to know if Muriel is seeing anyone?"

He looked up in surprise. Muriel Spencer was one of the non-sworn who answered phones down at the police station, and since she lived just up the block, she'd been casually flirting with his uncle for years. "As a matter of fact, she had a blind date last weekend that was so bad, she swore off men for good."

"Sounds like her. Well, I guess that's it then."

"'That's it?' You're not even gonna ask her?" Danny demanded, incredulous.

"Yeah," Garrett said, "I mean, she swears off men *every* time she has a bad date. And hell, she's waited on you long enough."

"What are you talking about?" The old guy's brow pulled together in confusion.

Could he possibly be that blind? "She's been waiting for you to ask her out for years."

"What? Why didn't you tell me? I'm not a mind reader."

"I did! And so did Sara. Don't you remember her telling you how handsome Muriel thought you were?"

"I remember. I just thought she was teasing. It never dawned on me..." A hopeful smile lit his face, making him look ten years younger. But just as quickly his expression fell. "Hell, who am I kidding? I haven't been on a date in almost four years. I'd bore her to death before we even finished our salads."

"Don't be silly, Uncle Luke. You'd do fine," Danny assured him as he rose to his feet. "Besides, she's already hot for you. That's half the battle right there."

Once Danny left, Garrett said, "So, you want me to get her number for you?"

Uncle Luke looked up, a twinkle in his eye. "Hell, why not? What's the worst that could happen? She turns me down? Not like I've never heard those words before."

Garrett laughed. "What man hasn't?"

"With that handsome mug of yours? Please, what woman would turn you down?"

"Jessica McGovern," he said, immediately wishing he could call the words back.

"Who?"

Garrett heaved a sigh, then got up to top off his coffee. "You know, Jessica. Charlie Peterson's niece. I have a feeling she'd hang up on me if I asked her out."

"Then ask her in person."

Yeah, when pigs fly. Garrett opened the cake box sitting on the counter and ran his finger through the frosting.

"So how about it?"

"How about what?" He stuck his icing-tipped finger in his mouth and closed his eyes in pure ecstasy. "I swear, Sara makes the best chocolate frosting I've ever tasted."

"Go ask the young lady out in person. I've seen you put on the charm when you want to. You could win her over if you put your mind to it."

Garrett lifted the cake out of the box, then pulled a knife from the butcher block. "Who says I'm interested anyway?" *You just did, you idiot.*

"Son, you can double-talk all you want. But I know you better than anyone, and there's no doubt in my mind you're interested."

"Well, you don't know me half as well as you think then 'cause, frankly, I'd rather date a rattler." *Probably be a whole lot safer with a rattler, too.*

"Is that why you talked about her all through supper?"

"I was telling you about my exciting afternoon," Garrett said, exasperated. "She just happened to be a part of it."

Uncle Luke leaned back against the counter and regarded him through concerned eyes.

With a slight shake of his head, Garrett set down the knife and pasted on a reassuring smile. "You worry too much. Listen, I'll make you a deal. The next time I see our new neighbor, if she isn't taking a swing at me, I'll ask her out. But then, next time you see Muriel, you have to ask *her* out. Deal?"

Uncle Luke grinned. "Deal."

Two

"You sneaky old man, you knew she'd be here," Garrett muttered the following afternoon as he led his uncle out onto the back patio of Mike and Sara's new home. He'd spotted Jessica immediately, sitting on a lawn chair chatting away with the neighbors from across the street.

And damn if she wasn't the sexiest sight he'd ever seen. Long, honey-blonde hair flowed in loose curls around her bare shoulders and down her back, a powder blue halter-top, several shades lighter than her eyes, emphasized ample breasts. And those gorgeous legs—what he wouldn't do to feel them wrapped around his waist—seemed to ooze out of a pair of well-worn Daisy Dukes.

"I knew Sara invited her, but I didn't figure she'd show up since she knew *you'd* be here." Uncle Luke pounded him on the back.

"Gee, thanks. Any more compliments like that and I may have to curl up in a corner and bawl my eyes out." Garrett turned on his heel and stepped back through the French doors into the living room.

Mike originally bought the big old house so he could be close to his son. But when he and Sara found their way back to each other, he promptly proposed and asked her and Ethan to move in with him. They decided to throw a small, combination housewarming/Fourth of July party so Mike could get to know a few of the neighbors.

"Hey, about time you guys got here." Garrett's younger brother, Nicky, walked out of the bathroom and made his way over. "Doesn't it blow your mind how much they've gotten done in three short weeks?"

"I like the new carpeting," Uncle Luke said as he stepped back inside. "It lightens the place up. That dark brown, retro shag old man Pankovich had made the place seem like a damn tomb."

"I agree," Garrett said, admiring the gleaming cherry banisters and baseboards, which looked brand new against the lighter shade of carpeting. "Who knew Mike would turn out to be such a handyman?"

"I heard that," Mike announced from the vicinity of the kitchen. He came out with three bottles of Michelob clutched in his hand and headed their way.

"You must've been reading my mind." He accepted the beer, twisted off the cap, and tilted it to his lips.

Mike cocked a brow. "Bad day?"

Before he could reply, Ethan ran into the house and raced straight for him. "Uncle Garrett, wait 'til you try the pool! It's awesome!"

He set his beer down, caught his nephew around the waist, and hauled him up to his shoulder. "Hey, sport. Having a good time?"

"Yep. Look how wrinkled my toes are."

Ethan stuck one foot up for inspection, almost kicking Garrett in the nose.

"Wow! You'll be lucky if those suckers ever get back to normal."

"I know, isn't it cool?"

He ruffled Ethan's hair, and then set him back on his feet. "So what did your mom make to eat? I'm starving."

"She made barbecued chicken, hamburgers...uh...baked beans. Some yucky stuff with noodles and peas—"

Garrett glanced at Mike.

"Macaroni salad."

"—and 'devil' eggs, and the stuff with lettuce and those black rings—"

He cocked a brow, and Mike grinned.

"Taco dip."

Ethan crossed his arms over his chest and peered up at Garrett. "Hey, if you eat, you can't go in the pool for like twenty minutes or you'll get stomach cramps."

"So come eat with me. Then we'll be able to jump in the pool at the same time."

His little face screwed up. "Oh, fine. But as soon as it's time, we're going swimming."

"Absolutely." He held out his hand. Ethan took it and squealed with delight as Garrett hauled him back up to his shoulder in one smooth motion. The two of them headed outside to the buffet table Sara had set up.

He smiled when he caught sight of Muriel.

"Hey, how's my favorite girl?"

The bubbly brunette tickled Ethan's feet. "Just fine. And how are the two best-looking men in Green Bay doing?"

"We're going swimming as soon as Uncle Garrett's done eating."

"Sounds like fun. So, did Luke come along, or is he home puttering around in the garage?"

Garrett grinned. "He's here. We walked down

together. As a matter-of-fact," he glanced toward the house and lowered his voice to a conspiratorial tone, "he asked about you last night."

Muriel's eyes grew big as hubcaps. "He did? Finally. Good God, I was starting to think the man was...you know."

He tipped his head back and laughed. "Ah, Muriel, Uncle Luke would've turned beet-red if he'd heard you say that. He's pretty darn shy, but he's not 'you know.' Why don't you break your own rule and go ask him out? He's old-fashioned, so it's not like he'd make you pay for dinner."

Muriel nibbled on her bottom lip and glanced toward the house. She was such an attractive woman, it surprised Garrett she was still single, even if her fiery personality did tend to scare most men off. She was petite, with big hazel eyes, shoulder-length nut-brown hair and a great rack. Garrett thought she looked closer to thirty than the forty-something he knew her to be.

"Maybe I will," she said with a gleam in her eye.

"Good. And I know just how you can break the ice."

Luke Jamison nearly choked on his beer when he saw Muriel strolling his way with a killer smile and a plateful of food. The lady was so beautiful he couldn't believe some lucky guy hadn't snapped her up already. She had a figure most women half her age would envy, and today, she wore a pair of those low-rise jeans with a white, spaghetti-strap tank top that featured the Led Zeppelin blimp.

Please, God, let something witty come out of my

mouth.

He cleared his throat and gestured toward her chest. "You know, I saw them once, but it was years ago."

"Oh, I don't think so." She grinned. "I would've remembered something like that."

Heat crawled up his neck. "I, uh…what I meant was...ah, hell, I'm an idiot."

"Actually, I think you're pretty cute. And I know what you meant, I was only teasing." She stopped in front of him and held out the plate. "Garrett asked me to bring this in to you."

"Thanks." He accepted it without making eye contact. *Chicken shit.*

"Don't mention it." She took a seat on the beige and gold flower-patterned sofa and patted the cushion beside her. "I'd be happy to keep you company while you eat."

"Maybe I should go eat this out on the patio. Sara'll skin me alive if I plop barbecue sauce on their new furniture."

"Relax, Luke. After four kids, trust me, I'm an expert at taking out stains."

With a hesitant nod, he walked over and sat down next to her, being careful not to sit too close. With his luck, he'd end up getting barbecue sauce on her as well as the sofa.

"So, how have you been?" she asked. "I haven't seen you down at the station in quite a while."

"I've been working a lot. Eating up the overtime." He picked up his fork and took a bite of the macaroni salad.

"Tasty, huh? Your Sara sure can cook." Muriel crossed her legs, her sandaled foot brushing his calf. "You know, I'm not a half-bad cook myself."

He glanced up after another bite of salad. "Can you

make pierogies?"

"My maiden name is Slotkowski; what do *you* think?"

He held her gaze for moment, even managed a small smile, before dropping his back to his plate.

Muriel took heart. Luke Jamison was easily the shyest man she'd ever met. And one of the best looking. He stood just shy of six-feet, had a thick, full head of salt and pepper hair with a matching mustache and beard that he kept neatly trimmed. Muscular, like his nephews, he was in surprisingly good shape for a man of nearly fifty. He wore a faded pair of Levi's with a black pocket T-shirt tucked into the waistband, which showed off a lean waist from all the years he'd spent doing hard physical labor at the paper mill. He had big, brown bedroom eyes, and some of the sexiest hands she'd ever seen.

Muriel had been itching to feel those hands on her since the moment they'd met.

He'd returned his attention to his plate, and more or less picked at his food. She decided to take it as a good sign, how uncomfortable he seemed around her. "I'd be happy to make those pierogies for you, Luke. Maybe you could come by my place for supper one of these nights?"

He looked up, his expression hopeful. "Really? I'd like that."

"It's a date then. What night's good for you?"

He shrugged. "Any."

"How about Friday? I'll make a pork roast and sauerkraut to go with the pierogies, and maybe we can watch a movie afterward?"

"Sounds good." He cleared his throat. "What time should I be there?"

His shy smile was a surprising turn on. "Five. That'll give us plenty of time for supper and a movie." *And if I pick up a bottle of wine, maybe a little more.*

"Five is perfect."

Muriel reached over and patted his thigh. "Great. I'm looking forward to it."

Jessica cast a quick glance at Garrett, who polished off his second plate of food while his nephew looked on with obvious annoyance. The guy was so hot and cold Jessica didn't know what to think of him. And so unlike the rest of his family.

She glanced at his sister, who happened to be one of the nicest people she'd ever met. "It amazes me *that* man is related to you."

"I know he can come off like a jerk sometimes," Sara Jamison admitted, "but I promise you won't find a more loyal, trustworthy guy." She grinned. "Once you get past all the thorns."

Jessica shrugged, less than convinced. "Sorry, but I've had my fingers pricked one too many times as it is."

"Well, that's a shame, because I happen to know he has a thing for you."

She snorted. "He wants to get in my pants."

"I'm sure." Sara grinned. "But it's more than that. Take it from someone who knows. He's practically burned a hole in the side of your head staring at you."

Jessica glanced back, and sure enough, he was watching her. When their eyes met, he quickly looked away. Jessica's brows rose. Could Sara be right? Did Garrett Jamison have more than a passing interest in her?

Im-frigging-possible. "Maybe he's wondering how much it would cost to have me euthanized," she mumbled under her breath.

"What?"

"Nothing. Just talking to myself." She plastered a smile on her face. "Listen, thanks for including me, but I think it's time I head home. I've got to work tomorrow and haven't touched my laundry yet."

Sara frowned. "You're not letting him run you off, are you?"

"Please, and give that man more power than he already *thinks* he has? No, honest, I have plenty to do at home."

"Good. And I'm glad you came by. Hope you enjoyed yourself." They both stood, and Sara gave her a hug. "Just promise you'll keep an open mind if Garrett ever does decide to reel you in."

Jessica chuckled. "*Reel* me in? Woman, you are long overdue for some female companionship."

"Where's she going?" Garrett asked his sister as Jessica disappeared into the house. He peeled off his T-shirt and stripped out of his jeans, revealing navy blue swim trunks beneath.

Ethan ran past with a loud "Outta my way!" and cannon-balled into the pool.

"She has to work tomorrow and had some chores to take care of."

"Hmmph."

"It's obvious you want her," Sara said. "Why not just turn on the charm and go get her?"

He scowled. "I don't want her. Hell, she's so bitter her lips probably taste like persimmons."

"So, you've been wondering what her lips taste like then?"

Garrett shook his head. "You've just got to romanticize everything, don't you?"

Her expression grew serious, and he just barely held back a sigh.

"I'm worried about you, big brother. You haven't been with anyone in a long time."

He let out an uncomfortable, half-hearted laugh. "Jesus, first Danny tells me I need to get laid, and now you?"

"I only meant dating, actually." She grinned up at him. "Men and women usually have different priorities when it comes to sex."

"Can't argue with that."

"So, are you going to ask her out or what? 'Cause if you're even half as interested as I think you are, you'd better get moving. That is one beautiful woman, and it won't be long before she's off the market."

Nicky walked up and joined them. "Hey, Sis. Do you happen to know if Charlie's niece is seeing anyone?"

Sara promptly burst out laughing.

"You two set that up," Garrett accused through narrowed eyes.

Sara held up a hand in disbelief. "I swear, it was a total coincidence."

"Set what up?" Nicky asked, frowning.

"You're moving to New York in less than two months," he pointed out, hating the surge of jealousy that tightened his chest.

"And I can't have a little fun before I go?"

"I don't give a shit what you do."

Nicky's knowing smile grated. "Sorry, big brother,

but I saw the way she looked at you. You'd have a better chance at a nun's convention."

"You two talk about her like she's a blow up doll," Sara snapped, her heated gaze ping-ponging between them, stopping on Nicky. "And I have news for you. You're not the one she wants."

He crossed his arms over his chest, his expression smug. "I know when a woman's into me. We chatted earlier, and she hung on every word I said."

"Yeah, to make this one jealous," Sara shot back, flipping her chin toward Garrett.

"What makes you so sure?" Garrett couldn't stop himself from asking. He grimaced at her shrewd smile.

"Bullshit."

Nicky cocked a brow in disbelief, and he wanted nothing more than to deck him at that moment.

"She actually told you she was interested in Captain Hothead here?" their brother asked. "Or is this some women's intuition crap."

Sara gave one of her 'men are clueless' eye rolls he'd become used to. "I don't need 'intuition' to know your name never came up in conversation." Her gaze centered back on Garrett. "And if your intentions are the same as Mr. Wham-bam's here, you can just forget it. She doesn't strike me as the casual sex type."

Jessica ran downstairs to pull the last load from the dryer, relieved to finally be done with laundry. She hadn't eaten much earlier at the party thanks to a nervous stomach, so she planned to fry herself up a big juicy cheeseburger. After supper, she'd soak in a hot bath for an hour or so, then get to bed early for a change. Though it did sort of suck to have to get to bed early on a Saturday.

There was a knock at the door just as she reached the top of the steps. She set the stack of towels on the back of the sofa and peeked out the window. Her traitorous body tingled with awareness when her eyes landed on her unwanted guest.

She swung the door open and said in her haughtiest tone, "What do *you* want?"

"I was hoping we could talk."

"About...?"

"Us."

Jessica laughed. "Jamison, I think you must've drank one too many beers at the party. There is no, nor will there ever be, an 'us.'"

Garrett's smug smile grated on her nerves. She tried to shut the door, but he quickly blocked her. Damn him and his cop reflexes.

"Why can't you just let me enjoy the rest of my night in peace?"

"I figure I owe you an apology. Not only for the restaurant scene, but for Ethan's behavior as well."

Jessica let out a lusty sigh. "I forgive you, okay?"

"Look," He propped his hands on his hips and stretched his neck from side to side. "I've had some...difficult things to deal with lately, and I've been inexcusably rude—mostly to you."

He grinned, and she was once again taken aback by that handsome mug of his. Especially his smile. Lord, the man was sexy.

"But when you hit me yesterday," he continued, "it was like you slapped the meanness right out of me."

"Well, I did put my shoulder into it."

He chuckled. "I was impressed, I'll tell you that."

She stared at him, struggling to come up with a way to shut the door without seeming rude.

"May I come in?"

Jessica chewed on the inside of her cheek, knowing she was entering dangerous territory if she let him in. She gave her head an 'I must be nuts' shake, then took a step back. "Fine. But don't think for one minute I'll be putting my cat out for you."

Following her inside, he admitted, "Hell, truth is, I don't mind cats. Though, I have a feeling yours won't want to come within ten feet of me."

"I swear, I've never seen him sit on someone's head before."

Garrett held his breath, afraid to fricken move. He'd taken a seat on the recliner, and as soon as he'd leaned his head back, her crazy cat hopped up and settled right atop his head, tail tickling his nose, back paws resting menacingly against the side of his face.

"He's going to scratch the shit out of me if I move, isn't he?" Garrett looked cross-eyed up at the cat.

"Well, you *have* threatened him every night this week, and Mr. Louie can be a bit of a grudge holder. You'll just have to wait until he gets bored and jumps off." She walked off into the kitchen. "Can I interest you in a cheeseburger?"

"Hell, cat, ever hear of an empty threat?" he muttered. To Jessica, he said, "Are you seriously not going to get this beast off my head?" He reached up and gingerly scratched under Mr. Louie's chin. To Garrett's amazement, the cat relaxed its back paws and started purring like a trolling motor.

"If you want to prove how sorry you are for acting like a jerk," Jessica was saying, "making nice with Mr. Louie is a good start. Like I said, he can be a bit of a grudge holder. Now, about that cheeseburger—"

With Mr. Louie wrapped around his neck like a mink stole, Garrett stood up and headed into the kitchen. "Sounds good to me."

Jessica whirled around. "Dammit, you almost gave me a heart attack!" Her eyes narrowed when they landed on Mr. Louie, then slowly softened as she watched him stroke the cat's head, its chin, its throat. Jessica licked her lips and slowly met his gaze.

"Keep looking at me like that and those burgers'll never get fried."

"Conceited jackass," she muttered, spinning back around.

He laughed and leaned up against her fridge. Mr. Louie continued to purr his little heart out as Garrett alternately stroked his head and scratched behind his ears. Jessica flipped the patties into the heated pan and started slicing up a tomato.

"So, why don't you tell me something about yourself. You've already met my entire family, and all I know about you is you're divorced."

"And it's a subject that's off-limits, got it?"

He frowned. "I'm not trying to pry, woman. Just curious."

Jessica glanced back over her shoulder and, once again, Garrett was struck by those beautiful blue eyes of hers. Almost the exact same color as the morning glories his sister planted along the back of the house.

"Sorry," she said, her shoulders losing some of their stiffness, her tone surprisingly contrite. "It's a touchy subject for me. And there's not much to tell about me, really. My mom and dad own a little coffee shop in Seattle where they've lived their whole lives. I have an older sister, Katie, who's twenty-seven, and a little brother, Richard, who just turned twenty-one."

"Sounds like a picture-perfect family."

She shrugged. "I think they're perfect. Katie teaches Tae Kwon Do, and Richard starts his third year at Michigan Tech this fall."

Feeling Mr. Louie completely relax, Garrett carefully unwrapped him from around his neck and set him on the floor. The cat angrily licked his paw, then took off as if shot from a cannon. "Michigan Tech, huh? Uncle Luke and I go ice fishing up that way every year. Portage Lake, outside of Houghton."

"Somehow, I can't picture you fishing. I mean, it takes a lot of patience if the fish aren't biting, and patience doesn't seem to be one of your strong suits."

She cast him a cheeky grin, and Garrett couldn't help but smile back. God, how he wanted her.

"Normally, it's not. But fishing is different. And don't ask me why, it just is."

He watched in silence while she piled sliced tomatoes, lettuce, ketchup, mustard, and even pickle chips onto a platter. She buttered the buns and placed them cut side down in a large non-stick fry pan.

"You really take your burgers seriously," he commented, stepping back so she could get into the fridge. She pulled out two bottles of iced tea and handed him one.

"A cheeseburger is just blah if the bun isn't toasted. Who wants to eat a blah cheeseburger?"

Garrett stared at her in silent contemplation as he shook the bottle. "Woman, you are one strange bird."

"I'm strange?" She let out a derisive laugh. "You threatened to skin my cat the other night, but *I'm* strange?"

"Touché." He twisted off the cap and gulped down half his tea before adding, "Maybe that's why we're so drawn to each other."

"Speak for yourself, Jamison. You're the one who keeps showing up wherever I am."

"And you love it." He set the bottle down on top of the fridge and strode forward, backing her up against the counter. "Admit it."

She lifted her chin a notch. "Actually, I was thinking your brother Nick's quite a catch. And he has a much sweeter disposition than you do."

"Nicky won't come within ten feet of you, if he knows what's good for him."

"You don't own me," was her childish retort.

Garrett didn't even bother with a response. He cupped her face in his hands and brought his mouth down on hers in a searing kiss.

THREE

It didn't take Jessica long to respond. Pulse racing, skin tingling, she opened her mouth and twined her arms around his neck.

Garrett slid his hands down to her waist and lifted her, depositing her on the counter top, never breaking the kiss. She breathed in the intoxicating scent of his aftershave, its spicy notes enveloping her like two loving arms. He spread her thighs and stepped between them.

Jessica moaned against his mouth and wrapped her legs around his hips, urging him closer still, meeting the thrust of his tongue with equal fervor. Garrett grasped her backside with both hands and squeezed, driving her wild with desire. He pulled her flush against him, his rock-hard erection nestled just where she wanted it most.

A suspicious smell made it past the fog surrounding Jessica's brain. She went still and sniffed the air, then tore her mouth from his with a squeal. "They're burning!" she cried, pushing against his chest as she wriggled to be free.

Garrett lifted her off the counter and set her on her feet. The nutty aroma of burnt butter filled the kitchen.

She snatched the fry pan off the burner and glowered up at him. "You made me burn my buns!" She pitched them in the garbage, set the pan in the sink, and turned on the faucet. The water crackled and hissed against the hot pan.

"So, why don't we take a ride to Cleaver's?" he suggested.

"Cleaver's?" She knew she was making the lippy pout-face, but didn't care. She turned off the burner under the hamburger patties and flipped those in the garbage as well. *Fairwell, my lovelies.*

You just had to let him inside, didn't you?

Hey, you're the one who kissed him.

Oh, shut the hell up, already.

As if reading her bat-shit crazy thoughts, the jackass grinned. "Yeah." He said. "They make a damn good burger, and their fries aren't bad either. Sound like a plan?"

Jessica's stomach let loose with a monster growl. Both frustrated and starving, her stomach won out. "Fine. But since this is your fault, you're buying."

"Man, I'm starving." Garrett took an appreciative whiff of the steaming paper bag as he held open Jessica's front door.

She cast him an incredulous look as she walked past him into the living room. "After all the food you wolfed down a few hours ago?" She set her purse on the coffee table and headed into the kitchen.

"It's been more than four hours," he countered, taking a seat on the recliner. After snitching a few fries from the bag, he added, "And I'm a big boy; I need more fuel than the average guy."

She returned, handing him a plate and a fresh bottle iced tea. "With a big head that requires a larger hat size than the average guy, too."

"Funny." Once she settled in the arm chair, he handed her a cheeseburger and order of fries, then dumped the bag over his own plate. "Guess Mr. Louie isn't the only grudge holder in this house."

"Sorry." She picked up the remote and clicked on the TV, running through the channels until Tom Cruise appeared on the screen. "Cool, *Jerry Maguire*."

"Don't tell me you like this guy?" Garrett scoffed. Christ, what was it with women and Tom Cruise? Sara thought the guy walked on water, too. "He's like four feet tall."

"He is not. You're just a giant," she shot back. "Everybody seems small compared to you."

"Please tell me you aren't going to make me watch this movie."

She rolled her eyes. "Fine, then you decide." She tossed him the remote.

Garrett caught it in mid-air and started flipping through the channels. He stopped on the movie *Striptease* with Demi Moore and glanced at Jessica with a questioning lift of his brow. "Not that I'm into strippers," he quickly explained, knowing how women felt about that kind of stuff, "but Burt Reynolds is a riot in this movie."

"I don't want to watch this," she said, looking oddly uncomfortable.

With a shrug, he kept flipping until he came across an episode of *Psych*.

Jessica nodded her approval.

By the time they finished eating, it was close to seven

o'clock. Jessica got up and carried their plates into the kitchen. "Well, Jamison, who would've thought we could spend this much time together without killing each other?"

"Hell, not me. Which reminds me, I'd like to know why you tried to separate my head from my shoulders yesterday in the restaurant."

Dead silence. Jessica returned to the living and met his gaze. "I told you, that subject is off-limits."

"You said the subject of your divorce was off limits, but you didn't slap me until after I made that comment about kids."

She sat down Indian-style on the floor next to the recliner, stroking Mr. Louie's back. "Look, I don't care to talk about my past. I'm not sure what else I can say to make you understand."

"I'm a pretty good listener, Jess. And anything you tell me would be strictly confidential. You have my word."

She looked up at him with those big blue eyes, and the temptation to pull her into his arms nearly overpowered him. Their earlier kiss had been cut short, and he hadn't been able to think about much since.

"There's nothing to tell," she insisted. "I got married too young, and he turned out to be a total loser. End of story."

Having hoped she would open up to him, Garrett felt a surprising sense of disappointment. "Fine. If that's the way you want it, I won't push." He swiped his fingers through his hair. "Your business is your business."

"Finally," she said with a playful roll of her eyes. "Listen, it's been great fun and all, but I have to get up early for work. So, if you wouldn't mind..." She gestured toward the door.

Garrett shook his head and chuckled. "Woman, you are hell on a man's ego."

"Somehow, I think you'll live."

"Well?" He stood up and motioned her forward. "Aren't you going to send me off with a good night kiss?"

She let out a delicate snort. "You act as if we're dating or something. Hell, we just got past our mutual dislike of each other."

"Is 'mutual dislike' what you were feeling when you wrapped your arms and legs around me in the kitchen?" he asked, annoyed by her casual attitude. "Because it's definitely not what I was feeling."

"I see your ego isn't as delicate as you thought it was."

Garrett reached down, grasped both her hands, and hauled her to her feet.

He gazed down at her, holding her tight against him with one hand, while the other worked the ponytail holder from her hair. Gently, he finger-combed the silky blonde tendrils away from her face while gazing down at her lips, fighting the urge to kiss her breathless.

"The hell with it," he whispered, losing the battle, and took her mouth with fierce possession.

Jessica melted into him without hesitation. She wrapped her arms around his neck and slanted her mouth beneath his, meeting the thrust of his tongue with a sexy little moan.

Garrett had to use every bit of his self-control to keep from stripping her naked and taking her right there on the floor. He wanted to taste every inch of her, make her burn for him, hunger for him. And she could deny it 'til the cows came home, but the way she responded to him was all the proof he needed—Jessica wanted him just as much.

Breaking off the kiss, he untwined her arms from around his neck and gently set her away from him. He was rock hard and throbbing, but he'd just made a decision. He wouldn't take her to bed until she admitted she wanted him. Call it stupid, or plain old male pride, but Garrett wasn't giving it up without some reciprocation of feelings.

Reciprocation of feelings? What the fuck's gotten into me?

His voice gruff, he said, "I'd better let you get to bed. To *sleep*."

Jessica cleared her throat and stepped back, arms crossed over her chest. Garrett wasn't sure if the gesture was self-protective, or to hide her nipples, which were hard and straining against the front of her halter-top. "Well, goodnight then."

With her lips red and swollen from his kisses, and her honey-blonde hair loose and tumbling around her shoulders, she was the sexiest sight he'd ever seen.

"Sweet dreams, Jess." He leaned down and kissed her on the forehead, then turned and strode out the door.

"Jamison, if you're sure this is what you want, I'll okay your leave. But I have to say, I think you're making a mistake."

Garrett stood over Captain Weinert's desk, hands on hips, heart in his stomach. Effective immediately, he was officially on a three-month leave from the force. "I appreciate your concern, Captain, but...I really need some time to get my head on straight."

The older man nodded his balding head in understanding. He rose to his feet and held out his hand. "You'll be missed. Give me a call when you 'get your head on straight,' understand?"

"You bet. Thank you, sir."

Garrett strode out of the office, down the corridor, and through the swinging front doors of the police station.

Heavy, gray rain clouds hung low in the sky, and by the time he reached his truck, a light drizzle had started.

He climbed in, but before he got his key in the ignition, a surge of panic hit him. Jesus, he felt nauseous. He laid his head against the steering wheel and blew out a hard breath. Leaving the force, even for a short time, was one of the hardest things he'd ever done. But he couldn't risk someone else getting hurt due to his carelessness. What if he made the wrong call again...

Heart heavy with uncertainty, he sat up, put the truck in gear, and headed home.

By the time Garrett pulled up in front of the house, it was nearly four-thirty, and the light drizzle had turned into a steady rain. He killed the engine and swung the door open in time to see Jessica dash barefoot across the front lawn to her own truck. She yanked open the door and rolled up the driver's side window so fast her head bobbed up and down with the motion.

The first genuine smile of the day tugged at his lips.

He slammed his own door and ran through the rain straight for her truck. Before she could utter a protest, he swept her up in his arms, hip-checked her door shut, and sprinted to her front porch.

"Now that's car side service!" Jessica grinned at him, her arms wrapped around his neck.

Garrett held her easily with one arm while opening the door with the other. "Someone's in a good mood today." He set her on her feet just inside her home.

After drying her feet on the carpet, she held onto his arm while slipping into a pair of fuzzy blue slippers. "I made over sixty dollars in tips today. Want some tea? I just put on a pot." She disappeared into the kitchen.

He wiped off his boots before following after her, his sullen mood dissipating in the face of her exuberance. "Sure. As long as it's not that nasty green stuff."

She waggled a familiar white tea bag at him. "Only the best for my company."

Garrett leaned back against the counter, crossing his arms and his booted feet. He watched Jessica move around the kitchen, pulling cups from the cupboard and milk from the fridge. Her gorgeous legs were encased in a slightly damp, skin-tight pair of well-worn jeans, her shapely ass just begging for his hands. She wore a red halter-top that crisscrossed over her ample cleavage. The wet, gauzy material clung to her breasts, leaving very little to the imagination. Garrett's hands clenched. Christ, how he wanted her.

He cleared his throat, grabbed a small, dog-shaped squeaky toy off the table, and started tossing it in the air. "I took a leave of absence from the force today."

Jessica stopped dead in her tracks and stared at him. "What? I don't understand. You love being a cop. Isn't that what you told me the other day?"

He caught the toy in his fist with a loud squeak, his gaze locked on her face. "It's complicated."

The teakettle whistled, breaking the tension. She gave

him one last considering look before turning to take care of the tea.

Garrett set the squeaky toy back on the table and came up behind her. She stiffened as he brushed against her and brought his hands up to rest on her bare shoulders. Her skin was warm and soft, and it took nearly all his self-control not to crush her in his arms.

He closed his eyes for a brief moment to get himself under control, only to have the flowery scent of her freshly washed hair assault his senses. It alarmed him how much he wanted her. How often he found himself thinking about her—fantasizing about her.

Slowly, he turned her to face him. He reached up and tucked a stray wisp of hair behind her ear. Her lips were parted, her cheeks slightly flushed. She was so incredibly beautiful, and some deep-seated instinct told him to turn tail and run as fast and as far as he could.

Instead, he leaned down for the kiss he'd been craving all week.

A knock at the back door broke the silence. Jessica pulled back just before their lips touched.

The rain drumming against the fiberglass awning that covered the back porch became louder as the door swung open. "Hey, Jess, sorry it took me so long. I got stuck on a phone conference with my new project manager in New York."

Nicky? Garrett swung around and scowled at his brother, who walked through the door as if he owned the place. "What the hell are you doing here?"

Jessica stepped around him and took Nicky's arm. "No problem. Your brother was kind enough to keep me company."

Nicky cocked a brow. "Garrett, kind? Don't hear

those words together in a sentence too often."

"Very funny," he groused. "Maybe you should take your act on the road."

Jessica frowned. "Be nice or you can both hit the road. And not that it's any of your business," she turned the full force of her annoyance on Garrett, "but I asked Nick to come over and show me how to work my word processor."

"Well, then *Nicky* can just march his ass back home, because I happen to know my way around a word processor well enough."

With a dismissive smile, Jessica informed him, "'Well enough' isn't good enough." She moved to the stove. "Nick, would you like a cup of tea?"

His brother strode past him with a smirk and took a seat at the table. "I'd *love* a cup, thanks."

Garrett glared at Nicky so hard it was a miracle he didn't burst into flames. He yanked a chair out from the table, spun it around and straddled it. On some level, it surprised him that his brother was acting like such an ass. He'd never purposely gone after a woman he knew Garrett was interested in—not that there'd been all that many. He could count on one hand the number of dates he'd been on in the past year, including a couple of one-nighters.

But he hadn't been this gut-twisted over a woman since high school. And Nicky had to know that.

"This is harder than I thought it'd be," Jessica admitted as she shut her laptop an hour later. "Sure wish I'd taken typing classes in high school."

Nick smiled at her. "Don't worry, you'll get the hang of it. Lots of people 'hunt and peck.'"

What a handsome guy, Jessica thought, not for the first time. Almost as handsome as his infuriating brother. She cast a quick glance at Garrett who glared daggers at the both of them.

"I don't know about that," she said, "but I appreciate your help. I'd like to make some extra money, and since I have a lot of spare time, I thought I'd give medical transcription a try."

"It won't make you rich, but it's nice to be able to work from home. And if you have any questions, give me a call. I don't leave for New York 'til the end of August."

Jessica followed Nick into the kitchen, Garrett right on her heels.

"That long, huh?" Garrett walked past them both and opened the back door. The rain fell even harder now, and the sky had darkened considerably.

Nick laughed and clapped his brother on the back. "Aw, come on, admit it. You're going to miss me."

"Yeah," Garrett grumbled, "like a hangover."

Shaking her head, Jessica walked up and kissed Nick on the cheek. "Thanks, I owe you." She could practically feel the heat of Garrett's displeasure. She wouldn't have taken him for the jealous type, but his possessive behavior couldn't be described as anything but.

And as much as she hated to admit it, having a man exhibit the green-eyed monster over her was a nice change.

"Careful, I just may take you up on that," Nick teased. Then he cast a quick glance up at the sky and dashed out the door.

Garrett swung the door shut with a muttered, "Good riddance."

Jessica rounded on him. "What in the world is your problem?"

"Don't play coy. You're using Nicky to piss me off, and you know it."

She stabbed a finger toward the door. "Get the hell out of my house, you arrogant jackass."

Garrett's jaw worked back and forth, his frustration evident. He took a step toward her.

Jessica held up a hand to ward him off. "Nuh-uh. I don't think so."

"Can't we just get back to where we were before Nicky got here?"

Even as annoyed as she was at that moment, Jessica's pulse sped up. Garrett Jamison was possibly the most obnoxious man on the planet, but she wanted him more than she'd ever wanted anyone. And that was exactly why she couldn't get involved with him. Her heart would end up on the line, and no way would she allow that to happen. Not again. Nope, she'd tried love and had failed miserably.

Unfortunately, she'd failed at pretty much everything else, too.

Even so, she dropped her hand, and Garrett reached for her, taking her in his arms. And Lord, how she wanted him to. More than anything, she wanted him to pick her up and carry her off to her bedroom. It had been so long since she'd felt the comfort of a lover's arms.

"I...I think maybe we should just keep things platonic. I don't want any complications in my life right now."

Garrett ran a gentle hand down her cheek to her chin,

along her throat, then slowly back up again. "I'm not asking you to marry me, Jess. But it's obvious we want each other. Why should we deny ourselves?"

He continued to tease the tender flesh just below her ear, and Jessica's eyes lowered in response.

She snapped them back open. "Sex can lead to other things. I don't want to hurt you, Garrett, but I'm serious when I say I don't want any complications in my life."

Frustration flickered across his face. "That makes two of us, then. All I was hoping for was some mutual satisfaction."

"Friends with benefits?" God, how she hated the sound of that.

He reached out again, but this time curled his big hand around the back of her neck and pulled her against his broad chest. "I couldn't have said it better myself." And then he captured her lips in a near savage kiss.

Jessica was saved from melting into a puddle on the floor by his strong arms. Meeting his questing tongue with mutual need, she reached up and twined her arms around his thick neck. Her nipples hardened; a groan rumbled up from deep in her chest. The man was a master kisser, no doubt about it. She felt helpless against his seductive assault.

Garrett slanted his mouth across hers, deepening the kiss. He smoothed one hand down her back until he reached her bottom, squeezing and lifting her against his erection. Jessica thought she might faint with desire as he continued plundering her mouth while his other hand cupped her breast. Another groaned escaped her as she moved to accommodate him, offering him her aching nipple. He found it through the gauzy material, teased and plucked until she was on the verge of begging him to put her out of her misery. She was wet and hot and wanted him so bad she'd started shaking.

Her phone rang, the shrill sound like an alarm going off in her lust-crazed mind.

Four

Jessica tore free of his lips with a muttered curse. Chests heaving, neither pulled back. They just stood there waiting—hard, wet, wanting.

The machine picked up and her mother's high-pitched voice filled the room. "Jess, honey? Are you home? This is important."

Recognizing the urgency in her mother's tone, she disentangled herself from Garrett's embrace and dashed for the phone.

"Hi, I'm here. What's going on?" She met his gaze with silent apology.

"He's been released!"

A slow buzzing started in her ears. She swallowed hard as a wave of nausea hit her.

Garrett strode toward her and mouthed, "What is it?"

Praying her face didn't betray her inner turmoil, she said, "Mom, hang on a sec." She covered the receiver and paused for a brief moment as panic set in. "I'm sorry. She, uh, needs to speak with me about some family business."

He didn't look happy, but neither did he complain. "Call you later?"

"I'll be here."

Garrett nodded and left through the back door.

Jessica took a deep, calming breath before lifting the phone back to her ear. "Mom, I couldn't have heard you—"

"They released him, Jess. I don't know how or when, but that man is out walking the streets again."

"All right, calm down. We knew this day would come." A surge of mixed emotions nearly buckled her knees—anger, confusion, shock, grief...fear—and the familiar, slow throb of a tension headache pulsed to life. She dropped down on the couch and closed her eyes.

"But not yet! He should have another year to serve." Her mom let out a long-suffering sigh. "Jessie, please, come home. I know things have been strained between you and your father, but he misses you and worries just as much as I do. We'll send you the money for airfare."

Her chest ached at the mention of her father. "There's no reason for you and Dad to worry. Wade has no idea where I am. And it's doubtful he'd care if he did."

"But you're all alone and have no idea what might be going through that man's mind. What if I came and stayed with you for a while?"

"I'm fine, Mom. I swear." Jessica massaged her temples with her free hand as the pounding in her head beat out of control. "Besides, there's a big cop who lives right next door. If I have any trouble, I can give him a call."

"That's right, I'd forgotten about him. What's his name again? Gary?"

She licked her lips. "Garrett. And yeah, he's...something else."

"Honey, promise me you'll give the officer a call if Wade tries to contact you. You know what a worrier I am."

"That may be the understatement of the century." Jessica could just picture her petite mother nervously chewing her nails as she paced back and forth across the hardwood floor in her favorite fuzzy slippers. A smile tried to break free, but all she managed was a grimace.

"Promise me."

She rolled her eyes. "I promise. If I need the cop, I'll call. Happy?"

"Happy. I'll be in touch soon."

Jessica pressed the receiver button and dropped the phone on the end table. *Wade's been released from prison.* The bastard hadn't even served half of his sentence, and he was walking around a free man? The injustice of it made her sick.

She nibbled on her thumbnail and started pacing the living room.

Okay, so what were the chances he'd show up in Green Bay? Better than she wanted to admit, frankly. The last time they'd stood face-to-face—before he'd been taken away in handcuffs—she'd told him they were through. Period. No chance in hell would she ever take him back.

Wade had sworn to change her mind when he got out.

"Remember, you promised to be good," Garrett reminded his nephew as he pulled open the door to the restaurant. "Any sass-mouth and I'll take you right home. I mean it."

Ethan frowned, but wisely nodded his head. He stomped through the door and stood next to the PLEASE

WAIT TO BE SEATED sign. Garrett couldn't help but grin. Even annoyed, Ethan had better self-control than his uncle.

The hostess, a busty, middle aged woman with a humongous salt-and-pepper beehive hairdo, walked up and chucked Ethan under the chin. "Hey, good-lookin', would you like a table or a booth?" She grabbed a menu, placemats, and a few crayons off the hostess stand.

"We'll take a booth," Garrett said. "In Jessica's section, if that's all right."

She cast him an appreciative once over and smiled. "She has a booth open in the corner. Follow me."

Ethan dragged his feet the entire way, then climbed in and crossed his arms, his little face screwed up in a mutinous scowl. Garrett let out a resigned sigh.

The hostess handed him the menu, set down the paper placemats, and dropped the crayons in front of Ethan. "Jessica will be with you in just a minute."

"I ain't no baby," Ethan muttered as soon as she walked away.

"You're seven, sport. There's nothing babyish about coloring when you're seven." Garrett flipped open his menu, hoping a decent meal might sweeten Ethan's disposition. Hell, who was he kidding? The only cure for his nephew's foul mood would be if Jessica disappeared from the planet. And *that* would surely put *him* in a foul mood. The thought of never seeing her again was enough to make his blood run cold. Damn, when did he become so attached?

He blew out a frustrated breath and glanced over the menu. "Hey, they have chicken quesadilla appetizers. Want to split an order?"

Ethan shrugged. "I s'pose." He picked up one of the

crayons and started doodling.

Garrett felt a glimmer of hope. He certainly didn't need the little squirt's permission to date Jessica, but it would be nice if he could at least be civil to her.

"Well, I didn't expect to see you two here."

Jessica approached the table, and Garrett had to clear his suddenly dry throat. Jesus, what in the world was wrong with him? It hadn't been *that* long since he'd gotten laid.

He shrugged. "We have to eat lunch, and this is as good a place as any." *Did that sound nonchalant enough?*

"So, what can I get you?" She pulled the pad and pen from her pocket before craning her neck to see what Ethan was drawing. "Wow, that's amazing. A dog?"

His nephew looked up with utter disdain. "It's a horse. Don't you know anything?"

Garrett's face grew hot with embarrassment. He slapped his menu shut and yanked the crayon from Ethan's grasp. "That's it, sport, I warned you. No lunch and no movies tonight. You can sit in your room and pout until you learn how to treat people with respect." His gaze moved to Jessica. Jesus, what she must think. "I'm sorry. I honestly thought his manners would've improved by now."

Ethan's eyes grew red and his chin quivered. "But it's a horse! Anyone can see that!"

Garrett had had enough. He started to push himself to his feet when Jessica laid a placating hand on his forearm.

"Please, he's right. Anyone can see it's a horse. I don't know what I was thinking." She then turned to Ethan. "You know, we make one of the best cheeseburgers in the city, and it comes with a big plateful of curly fries. *And* if you finish your food, you get a free sundae. What do you think? Are you up for it?"

Ethan shrugged a shoulder, but remained silent.

"If you don't think you can do it..." Jessica added, letting her words trail off as if in silent dare.

Garrett watched in wonder as most of the hostility faded from his nephew's eyes. The thrill of possible victory even brought a smug grin to the little shit's face. A free sundae? There wasn't much Ethan wouldn't do for that.

"Well, sport, it's up to you. Do we stay, practice our manners, and have one of the best cheeseburgers in the city, or go home for some of Uncle Luke's Spam casserole?"

Ethan shivered in revulsion. Garrett and Jessica both laughed.

"I guess that settles it. And I think I'd like to try that challenge as well." He handed Jessica both menus as he mouthed the word "thanks".

She winked. "Okay, so that's two cheeseburger challenges. What can I get you to drink?"

Ethan glanced at Garrett who nodded. Those bright blue eyes lit up. "A large orange soda. And no onions on my cheeseburger."

"Make it two sodas." Garrett leaned back and laid his arm along the back of the booth. "And no onions on mine either." He returned her wink.

She rolled her eyes, but he caught a hint of a smile as she turned away.

Thirty minutes later, Jessica set two huge, cherry-topped hot fudge sundaes on the table with a flourish. "I have to say, I'm impressed. You boys sure can eat." Of course, she'd never admit she'd seen Garrett filching curly fries off his nephew's plate. The kid was, after all, only seven.

And while Ethan wasn't exactly smiling and friendly, he *had* managed to refrain from hurling insults at her. For that, she was grateful.

"Yeah, but nobody can eat as much as Uncle Danny," Ethan informed her. "I saw him eat a whole cake before."

Jessica widened her eyes dramatically. "No way! A *whole* cake? He must've had a bellyache for a week."

He nodded, warming to his subject. "Yep, and he puked his guts up, too."

"Ethan, we're in a restaurant," Garrett warned in a low tone. He met her gaze and shook his head. "Sorry."

Jessica waved his worry away. Although a typically indulgent and caring uncle, Garrett didn't let the little stinker get away with bad behavior, which, she had to admit, was another check in the man's 'pro' column.

She slid the check face down onto the table and said, "Well, I'm glad you guys stopped in for lunch. Have a great time at the movies tonight. Eat some popcorn for me."

Garrett cocked a brow at his nephew whose little face screwed up in resignation. "If you wanna come, you can come," Ethan grudgingly invited. "But you have to eat your own popcorn."

He earned a smile from his uncle, which seemed to please him.

Jessica knew the last thing Ethan wanted was for her to tag along, though, and decided there was no point in pressing her luck. They'd be neighbors for at least five more months, and it would certainly be easier for everyone if Ethan didn't think of her as the Wicked

Witch of the West.

"Thanks. I appreciate the offer, I really do. But the last thing I want to do is intrude on a guys' night out."

Garrett raised both brows at his nephew this time, and Ethan set his spoon down with a resigned sigh. But when he glanced back up at her, his smile seemed almost genuine. "It's okay. My mom even comes with us on guys' night out sometimes. And she's a girl, too."

Jessica could barely hold back a giggle. She looked over and met Garrett's gaze with a you-don't-have-to-do-this look. But the truth was, she hadn't been to a movie theater since she was a kid, and, darn it, she wanted to go.

"Come on, it'll be fun," Garrett said. "We're going to see that new superhero movie. And it'll be my treat, popcorn and all."

She glanced back and forth between them. "If you're sure I'm not intruding, I'd love to come. I haven't seen the inside of a theater in years."

Ethan shoved a heaping spoonful of ice cream into his mouth and shook his head. "We're not going to the theater," he said after gulping it down. "We're going to the drive-in!"

Jessica gazed around at the sea of cars, mini-vans and pickup trucks feeling like a little kid who'd just discovered Disneyland. Dusk settled over the expansive gravel lot as Garrett parked his truck in the row closest to the big white screen, but off to the side. For now, they had the entire front row completely to themselves.

Smiling, she unbuckled her seatbelt and turned back

to face Ethan. "Thanks again for inviting me to come along. You didn't have to, and I would've understood if you hadn't."

His cheeks pinkened, and Jessica's smile widened.

"It's no big deal. But..." He cocked a brow. "You have to stay in the truck with Uncle Garrett. I want the hood all to myself."

She glanced over at Garrett who winked at her.

"Don't worry, sport, I'll make sure she stays in here with me."

Ten minutes later, lying on a pillow and blanket on top of the hood, Ethan wiggled his sneaker-clad feet in time with the dancing soda pop, candy, popcorn, and ice cream bars. And since he'd situated himself directly in the middle, Jessica had to either sit against the passenger door, or squeeze up against Garrett's side. Of course, she'd love to curl up in his arms to watch the movie, and doubted he would voice any protests. But she had a feeling Ethan wouldn't like it too much.

Garrett reached in back and grabbed a couple cans of soda from the small cooler he'd brought along. "Root beer?"

"Sure, thanks."

He wiped the condensation off on his jeans before handing her one, then repeated the process with his own. Jessica pulled the tab and took a small sip, while Garrett sucked down half the can in one long gulp. They glanced at each other, smiled, then looked away.

Garrett chuckled and scooched down in his seat, his long legs spread out, his knee practically touching her thigh. "I feel like I'm sixteen years old again, out on my first date."

Jessica couldn't help but laugh. "Actually, this is

much better. I had my first date at the roller rink. I was about the worst skater around, too, let me tell you."

He glanced at her, then returned his attention to the big screen. "Come on, you couldn't have been that bad."

She took another sip of her soda before leaning her head back against the headrest. "We were holding hands, and he skated backwards while I skated forwards. He basically pulled me around the rink 'til we'd built up quite a bit of momentum. I got scared, tried to use the toe stop and tripped. I'm told it looked like I did a dive-and-roll into two old ladies who were unfortunate enough to be standing right in front of the exit from the rink."

Garrett threw back his head and howled with laughter.

Her lips twitched. "It's not that funny." She saw Ethan turn back and frown at them through the windshield. She gave Garrett's knee a quick slap.

He managed to take it down to a snicker before turning to face her. The sun had completely set, but his handsome face was illuminated by the reflection off the big screen. His gaze slid down to her lips, and she licked them in reflex. Good Lord, the man could turn her into a toasted marshmallow with one smoldering look.

"Were they hurt?"

"Huh?"

He chuckled softly. "The little old ladies."

"Oh, they were fine. Just got knocked on their butts. I, on the other hand, skidded across the carpet on my face. Ended up with a quarter-sized rug burn on my chin. Probably looked like a monster zit from a distance—and if you laugh, I swear I'll dump this can over your head." She held up her root beer and playfully narrowed her eyes.

"Woman, I love your gall," he said, "but if even one

drop of that gets spilled in my truck, I'll pull you across my knee."

"That doesn't exactly sound like punishment."

He reached out and brushed his knuckles down her cheek, the pad of his thumb gently sweeping across her lips. Jessica's nipples tightened and her breath hitched. It scared her how easily his touch affected her. Even Wade, her first love and who was as handsome as they came, had never evoked such intense feelings. Jessica wanted to strip Garrett naked and have her way with him right there in the truck. And if Ethan wasn't with them, she'd probably be sitting on his lap right now—sans shorts and panties.

She squeezed her eyes shut and took a deep, shuddering breath.

"You okay?" he whispered.

Jessica realized he'd slid over until they sat thigh to thigh. She cleared her throat and made a big production out of reaching for her soda to dislodge his hand from her face. "I'm fine. The movie's about to start."

He flashed his teeth and slid back over. "Sorry. Wouldn't want you to miss the opening credits."

"Or have Ethan glance back and get an eyeful. I doubt I'd get another invite to the movies if he caught me lying across your lap. And actually, this is kind of fun."

"It'd be even more fun if you were lying across my lap."

Garrett's deep sexy voice washed over her like a hot caress. She squeezed her knees together and, with a silent sigh, settled in to watch the movie.

Garrett couldn't keep his eyes off of Jessica. Thank God the movie was over. He could get out of the truck, stretch his legs, and cool the hell down. Sitting there in her turquoise tank top and matching shorts, blonde hair pulled up into an *I Dream of Jeannie* ponytail, those delectable tan legs pressed together as if in silent warning, she was as tempting a sight as ever. He wanted to slide his hand between those silken legs and gently pry them apart. He'd been sitting with a semi-hard-on for most of the movie.

Ethan sat up and slid off the hood. He came around to Garrett's side of the truck and announced, "I gotta pee."

Garrett turned to Jessica. "We've got some time before the next movie starts. Come on, I've got a taste for dried up pizza and stale nachos."

She laughed and grabbed her purse. "Mmmm, you sure know how to spoil a girl."

Fifteen minutes later, they found their way back to the truck.

"Uncle Garrett, I'm tired. Can I watch the other movie from the backseat? Just in case I fall asleep. I'm afraid I'll slide off the hood."

He chuckled and ruffled Ethan's hair. "Sure. I already tossed your pillow and blanket back there, so go ahead and snuggle up."

Less than halfway through the second movie, soft snores could be heard from the back seat. Garrett leaned over and made sure Ethan didn't have a can of soda or candy in his hand before covering him up with the blanket.

Feeling Jessica's eyes on him, he dropped back into his seat and turned to face her. "Amazing he lasted this long. He usually conks out five minutes after the restroom break."

"With a bellyful of soda and stale nachos?"

"Yep. It's like taking sleeping pills."

"You're teasing me."

He cast one last glance over his shoulder before reaching out and capturing her hand. "I don't tease."

Jessica's breath caught when Garrett's big, warm hand wrapped around hers. He'd been a perfect gentleman all night, but now that Ethan was sleeping, she had a feeling he was done holding back. And truth be told, she'd been aching to feel his arms around her, to feel his warm lips on hers. Thank God for tinted windows.

He turned to face her, his thumb stroking her fingers as he reached out and caught her chin with his other hand. "Come here."

Good Lord, that deep voice would be the death of her yet.

"Aren't you afraid Ethan will wake up?" she whispered, even as she scooted toward him.

"Nope. The boy sleeps like the dead, trust me."

The spicy, masculine scent of his aftershave washed over her the moment he captured her lips. A soft moan escaped her. The man looked sexy, spoke sexy, smelled sexy. And he could knock her socks off with just one hot, wet kiss.

Jessica leaned forward as his arms closed around her, enveloping her in his warmth. Before she knew it, she was sprawled across his lap, her arms twined around his neck as he plundered her mouth. She could feel his erection, hard and unyielding beneath her, and couldn't stop herself from moving against him.

Garrett let out a groan as he brought his right leg up

onto the seat and clutched her behind with both hands. He kneaded the soft flesh, molding her against him as he leaned back in a more comfortable position. His tongue continued its exquisite assault on her mouth as his hands wreaked havoc on her senses. Before she knew what he was about, he slid his hands beneath the waistbands of both her shorts and panties and gripped her backside again, warm palms against her needy flesh.

Wet, aching, and mindless with wanting him, Jessica nearly sobbed by the time he brought a hand up to cup her breast, teasing her straining nipple through the fabric of her tank top and bra. She tore her lips from his and buried her face in the crook of his neck. With one hand holding her firmly against his erection, and the other stroking her nipple, driving her to near madness, Jessica wondered if it was possible to die from pure, intense pleasure.

"I want to taste you," he whispered, releasing his grip on her bottom to reach up and cup both her breasts.

She leaned back and met his heavy-lidded gaze before lifting her tank top and unclasping her front-hooking bra, freeing her breasts for his hungry perusal. When his hot mouth closed over one pebbled nipple, Jessica rolled her head back on her shoulders with a shuddering sigh.

"Uncle Garrett?"

FIVE

Jessica fell to the floor of the truck with a squawk of dismay. Garrett cleared his throat, swiped his fingers through his hair. "Hey, sport, I thought you were sleeping," he said in a comically high voice.

She hurried to get her bra clasped, and just managed to pull her tank top down by the time Ethan's head popped up above the seat. His eyes went immediately to her.

"Did you drop your Milk Duds?" he said, surprising the heck out of her.

"Uh, yeah. That's exactly what I did," she said, pretending to look around on the floor. She glanced up at Garrett who was leaning forward with his elbows on his knees, eyes squeezed shut, sucking in deep silent breaths as if trying to will that sucker down. Jessica had to bite down on her bottom lip to keep from laughing at the scene.

"I did that last time, that's how I knew," Ethan remarked before letting out a huge yawn.

His head disappeared, and Jessica blew out a sigh of relief before climbing back up onto the seat.

She scooted as close to the passenger-side door as she possibly could, then crossed her left leg over her right as an extra security measure.

Garrett finally sat up straight and craned his neck around to look down on Ethan. His expression wry, he said, "Out like a light again. Can you believe it?"

She shook her head and let out a soft snort. "Even in his sleep the little stinker doesn't want us together."

An hour and a half later, Garrett pulled the truck up in front of his house and killed the engine. He hesitated, then leaned back against the door and turned to face her. "Let me make this up to you. Dinner, just the two of us, the restaurant of your choice."

She peered up through her lashes. Now that she'd had a chance to cool down and think straight, she realized her feelings for the big oaf were stronger than she'd thought. And it scared the hell out of her.

After her divorce became final, she'd decided she was through putting her heart on the line. If she wanted a man, she'd have him, but with no strings attached. Jessica had learned the hard way how much blind love could cost you.

"I don't know...maybe your nephew is on to something. I mean, we got so carried away, we almost...with him right in the truck. You touch me, and my morals go right out the window. I'm sorry, but I don't think this 'friends with benefits' thing is going to work."

Moonlight washed across his face and she could make out the frustration in his expression.

"Believe me, I'm as disappointed with myself as you are. But we want each other. We're both going into this with eyes wide open. Other than making sure we're alone next time, I don't understand what the problem is."

The problem is, I think I'm already half in love with you. "Look, I'm beat. Can we talk about it tomorrow?"

Garrett blew out a heavy breath. He got out of the truck and came around to open her door.

"I really did have a nice time tonight," she said. "Thanks for letting me tag along."

"Glad you enjoyed yourself."

She couldn't help but smile. "A little too much. Thank God Ethan woke up when he did. If he'd have been ten minutes later..."

Garrett leaned down and whispered in her ear, "I'd have been inside you."

Her breath caught. She bit her bottom lip and leaned into his warmth. The man was a master of seduction, no doubt about it.

She cleared her throat and took a step back. "Goodnight. Thanks again...for everything." Without waiting for a response, Jessica dashed across the lawn to the sanctuary of her front porch.

As she searched around the bottom of her purse for her keys, she watched Garrett lovingly cradle Ethan in his arms and carry him into the house. Now, how in the world was she supposed to have a purely sexual relationship with a man who evoked such strong feelings of home, hearth, and family?

With a reluctant sigh, she opened the door and dragged her tired bones inside.

Thank God she had the next day off, because she planned to climb into bed and sleep the entire day away.

The pounding started at eight a.m. Jessica cracked an eye open and scowled at her alarm clock. Who the hell could be inconsiderate enough to use a hammer this early in the morning? Who in their right mind—

"Uncle Garrett, I found the other hammer!"

Jessica flopped onto her back and let out a curse that would have earned her a pinch on the arm from Grandma McGovern. *Well, doesn't that just figure?* Hadn't she suffered through enough torture with the big gorgeous jerk making an appearance in every dream she'd had? Morphing from the delivery guy at the restaurant, to the man behind the counter at the gas station, to the hunk who'd taken her fast-food order last weekend.

The hammering slowly grew louder and faster. Giving up any hope of sleeping the morning away, Jessica threw the sheet aside and flounced from the bed. She stalked into the kitchen to put on a pot of water for tea, then ran into the bathroom to brush her teeth, wash her face, and run a brush through her hair.

Halfway through her second cup, a rap sounded on the screen door.

"Hey, Jess, you awake?" Garrett shouted.

She rolled her eyes and turned to glower at the back door. Maybe if she kept quiet, he'd get bored and go away.

"Jess? Come on, sweetheart, you don't plan to sleep all day, do you?"

Sleep all d—? *What a jackass!*

She set her mug down with a thud, stormed to the back door, and swung it open. "I'd love to know how a person can"—she made air quotes—"sleep all day when her inconsiderate neighbor is pounding away in the backyard. Just what in the world are you two doing back there anyway?"

Garrett grinned, fueling her anger. When she tried to slam the door in his face, he yanked open the screen and stepped inside.

"Can't you just go away and leave me alone?"

She plopped down on a chair and swiped up her mug of tea. Reluctantly, she admired the skintight fit of the black T-shirt stretched across his broad chest. He wore an old pair of holey, faded Levi's, and sexy black biker boots.

Garrett spun the chair next to hers around and straddled it. When a whole minute of silence went by, she looked up and snapped, "Well, what is it? Why are you just sitting there gawking at me?"

"You're not exactly a morning person, are you?" He flipped open the box of powdered sugar donuts sitting on her kitchen table and helped himself to the last one. He wolfed it down then had the nerve to comment, "Sara's are much better. You shouldn't waste your money on the packaged kind."

Jessica shot to her feet and jabbed a finger toward the door. "Get out! Right now, I mean it!"

The infuriating man had the gall to smile. Jessica was about two seconds away from dumping her tea on his head—even if she had to climb up on her chair to do it.

"Listen, I just came by to see if I could take you out to dinner tonight. There's a nice Italian restaurant over on Twelfth Avenue that makes the best Chicken Parmesan I've ever had. Don't tell Sara I said that," he added in a conspiratorial whisper.

She pinned him with her most disgruntled look and let out a hearty sigh. "If I say yes, will you leave?"

Garrett rose to his feet and turned the chair back around. Mr. Louie chose that moment to drop down from his perch on the windowsill and start circling figure eights between Garrett's legs.

"Glad to see someone's in a good mood this morning." He reached down to scratch Mr. Louie behind the ears.

Jessica swore she could feel her blood pressure rising. "I was in a great mood until *someone* started hammering at eight o'clock in the morning!"

He straightened and grasped her forearm. "Come here, Miss Crabbypants."

She resisted, but it was no use. The big oaf outweighed her by a ton.

"Look, I just want to finish my tea and relax. Today's my last day off for almost two weeks."

He leaned back and frowned down at her. "Why are you working so many hours?"

Jessica rolled her eyes. "Um, I have bills to pay...?"

His gaze became pensive as he massaged the back of her neck. Slowly, she relaxed until she was leaning into his broad chest, eyes closed, inhaling his spicy masculine scent. He always smelled so good...Damn, the man was a magician; she'd already forgotten why she was mad at him...*Wait, oh yeah.* "So what's with all that hammering?"

"We're building a doghouse."

His busy fingers moved to her shoulders wringing a groan of ecstasy from her. Oh, God, was she drooling on his shirt? Then his words registered.

Jessica leaned back and swiped her mouth with the back of her wrist. "A doghouse? But you don't have a dog...do you?"

"No, but Ethan's been begging for a puppy for a couple years now. I guess he finally wore Sara down. And Mike's still in the 'buy-Ethan-anything-he-wants' phase." Garrett glanced down at the wet spot on his T-shirt and chuckled. He reached out and recaptured the back of her neck. "Liked that, did you? You do seem a little tense—"

"Oh, no you don't." She ducked out of his reach and took a few steps back. He started to follow but she held up both hands. "You stay right where you are."

He propped his hands on his hips. "So, do I have a date tonight or what?"

"Or what."

"Wear something sexy," he ordered before strolling out the back door.

The jackass even had the nerve to whistle.

Jessica walked over and slammed the door with a muttered, "Nutjob." Then she headed into the bedroom to search through her closet.

"Make yourself comfortable, Montgomery," the prison guard advised as the cell door slammed shut. The clip of his heels against the concrete faded away as he disappeared down the corridor.

"So, what are you in for?"

Jack Sutton cracked one eye open and glared up at the idiot who'd just been let into the cell. In less than five hours, he'd walk out of this place a free man, and all he wanted to do until then was sleep. He dismissed the balding, weasel-faced slug with a grunt and rolled over to face the wall. The guy took a piss, flushed the toilet, then cross the small cell and climb up onto the top bunk.

"I just transferred over from the hospital," Montgomery said. "Got shot in the chest by a cop."

"Do I look like I give a shit?"

"Sorry, man, I'm just a little nervous. Ain't never been in the joint before," the idiot admitted. "I shot a cop, but he's fine. I just winged him. Big guy like that don't go down easy, I'll tell you that."

Jack cracked an eye open again, this time with interest. "Oh yeah? How big?"

"Shit, I bet the dude's at least six-and-a-half feet tall," Montgomery said, his need to brag obvious. "One of those muscle heads, with arms as thick as my legs."

Jack rolled back over and laced his fingers behind his head. "So, what in the world made you shoot at a cop? You got a death wish or something?"

"I had no choice. I got mixed up with this other asshole cop who got burned by Jamison's sister."

His mouth went dry. No goddamn way. "Jamison?" he repeated, keeping his tone even. No way could this idiot be talking about the same cop who'd helped put Jack behind bars. Officer Jamison had been big, but not *that* big. Seven years had gone by, though. People change in seven years.

The bunk squeaked as Montgomery shifted. "That's the cop. The one I shot. His sister was dating the other cop and seeing her ex at the same time. Believe me, it didn't go over well."

"Are you saying some cop wanted Jamison dead just because his sister was screwing around on him?"

"Nah, that was only part of it. He knew Jamison was on to him."

Jack rubbed his eyes, hard. "On to him how?"

More shifting and squeaking. "He found out Thomas was dealing drugs."

Huh. Very interesting. "So, where did all this happen? Right here in Green Bay?"

"Yep."

A slow smile spread across Jack's face. Seven years. He'd spent seven long, miserable years behind bars for a crime he didn't commit. For a crime he hadn't had a thing to do with. And Officer Jamison's testimony had hammered the nail in his coffin.

Maybe Jack should return the favor.

Garrett scowled as Sara slapped his hands away and worked out the knot he'd made of his necktie.

"Here, let me do it. I swear, I've never seen you this nervous."

"I'm not nervous," he hotly denied. "I just don't like wearing ties." He glanced over at his brother-in-law-to-be who watched with an amused smirk. "Mike, do me a favor and take her home."

Mike chuckled. "Sorry, buddy, but this is the most fun I've had in days."

His sister turned to glare at her fiancé, and it was Garrett's turn to chuckle. "And it looks like it'll stay that way, *buddy*."

Sara gave his tie a yank. "Shut up and stand still."

Garrett studied his sister's face as she concentrated on his tie. He frowned when it dawned on him just how pasty she looked. "You feeling okay?"

"I'm fine, why?" She glanced up before casting a quick peek at Mike.

"I don't know. You don't look so good."

She snorted. "Gee, thanks a lot."

"You know what I mean. You look...tired." He sent Mike an accusatory look. "Have you been letting her work too hard?"

Mike walked over and gently grasped Sara's chin, turning her to face him. His brow creased. "He's right. You're pale as a ghost."

Sara shook off his hand. "Exaggerate much?"

"When we get home, you're going straight to bed."

Ignoring him, she went back to straightening Garrett's tie.

"Sorry, Sis, but I agree with Mike. You need some rest. And maybe a good meal. Have you eaten today? I could make you a quick fried egg sandwich—"

Sara went from pale to green, then took off like a shot into the bathroom. When the sound of retching reached his ears, Garrett shot a look at Mike, who ran after her. They returned a couple minutes later. Mike had his arm wrapped around her, and Sara could barely meet Garrett's gaze.

"All right, what the hell's going on? You love fried egg—"

His sister held up a hand as if to ward off his words. She looked ready to race back into the bathroom. Garrett exchanged a worried look with Mike.

Sara rolled her eyes, plopped down on the couch and admitted, "I'm pregnant."

"What?" Mike and Garrett shouted in unison.

She dropped her head into her hands and nodded. "I took a test this morning. God, I don't remember being this sick with Ethan," she muttered.

Mike sat down next to his fiancée and rubbed her back, his face a mask of pure shock. "When in the world were you planning on telling me? Christ, Sara, you don't just spring this news on a guy like—"

Her head whipped around and she looked on the

verge of tears. "What are you saying? Don't you want this baby?"

"Sweetheart, of course I do," Mike insisted, his voice gentle. "It's just...I was hoping we'd be married before any more kids came along." He stood up and helped Sara to her feet.

Eyes red-rimmed, she told Garrett, "Your tie is still crooked."

He walked up and kissed her on the top of her head. "I'm thrilled for you. And everyone else will be, too. But right now, I think you should let Mike take you home. You really do need to lie down."

She let out a watery, half-hearted laugh. "As much as I hate to agree with you, I think you're right. I feel like I could sleep for a week."

"Come on, honey, let's get you home," Mike said, wrapping his arm around her again. "And after your nap, we have a wedding to plan."

Sara gazed up at Mike with the most beautiful smile Garrett had ever seen. A surprising surge of emotion struck him, rendering him unable to speak.

At the door, she turned around and said, "Garrett, I want to be the one to tell everyone, particularly Ethan. I'm a little afraid of how he'll react. He's been acting awfully possessive of Mike." A small grin curved her lips. "Yesterday, he told the woman behind the counter at the bank that his mommy didn't like it when other girls smiled at his daddy."

Garrett couldn't help but laugh. He cast a quick glance toward the basement steps to make sure the little shit wasn't eavesdropping before remembering Nicky had taken him out for ice cream. "Yeah, he's been a little less than friendly with Jessica, too."

Mike and Sara shared a look and a chuckle then said in unison. "We heard."

"Have a great time tonight," she added, before letting her fiancé escort her out the door.

Garrett released a heavy sigh as he watched them head home. He was thrilled for the two of them, he truly was. But a surprising punch of jealousy had nailed him square in the gut when Sara dropped her little bombshell. He hadn't realized until just that moment how much he craved a family of his own. As he grabbed his keys off the end table, he envisioned a little girl with a moppet of honey-blonde curls and big blue eyes running around the house, her smile as breathtaking as it was devilish.

And she was the spitting image of his ornery next-door neighbor.

Giving his head a shake, Garrett checked his back pocket for his wallet, took one last shot at straightening his tie, then headed out the door.

Already waiting for him on the front porch, Jessica's ruby red lips were pursed in what seemed to be...uncertainty? No way. She looked gorgeous and had to know it. A woman couldn't be that beautiful and not know it.

The sun was still bright in the sky, and he wasn't sure if his knees would hold up by the time he reached her. He devoured her with his gaze from head to toe—it was all he could do not to run up, throw her over his shoulder, and carry her into the house.

"Hi," she said. She tugged at one of her earrings, a small gold hoop with a teardrop-shaped pearl hanging from it, and looked everywhere but at him.

He felt a measure of male satisfaction that she'd taken his "wear something sexy" comment to heart. She'd pulled her hair up into a loose bun with stray golden wisps left loose to frame her face. A necklace that matched her earrings hung from her throat and nestled just above her full cleavage. She wore a strapless little black number that hugged her curves and ended just above her knees. And her dainty feet were encased in a sparkly pair of silver sandals, the heels at least three-inches high. He grinned. Even with the added height, she barely reached his chin.

"You look incredible," he said, stepping up onto the porch.

"Thanks. You don't look half bad yourself."

Garrett reached out and gently captured her chin between his thumb and forefinger. "Careful, such flattery might go to my head," he teased.

"Heck, Jamison, that sucker barely fits through the door as it is."

He chuckled and dropped his hand. "Good thing I've got a thick skin."

"You know I'm teasing."

Garrett couldn't help himself. He leaned down and kissed her. A quick, gentle kiss that only left him yearning for more. He cleared his throat. "Well, we'd best get going. I made the reservation for seven-thirty and it's nearly ten after now."

She grabbed her purse and a silky black shawl and grasped his elbow. "I'm ready. Let's go."

Smiling as he escorted her to his truck, Garrett had no doubt this would be a night to remember.

"Would you like a taste?"

Jessica leaned closer so Garrett could feed her a bite of the homemade cannoli he'd ordered for dessert. Her eyes closed in pure ecstasy. The creamy, cinnamon-ricotta filling with bits of chocolate, the crispy shell...mmmm. Cannoli had just become her new favorite dessert.

"Good, huh?" he said, his voice low and erotic, sending a shiver of awareness straight down to her toes.

"Delicious. In fact, the entire meal was the best I've ever had."

She meant it, too. The fettuccine with grilled chicken, sun-dried tomatoes and baby artichokes was, without a doubt, the best pasta dish she'd ever eaten. And the ambiance of the restaurant was wonderful. The dim lighting and soft music created a romantic atmosphere, while the gold-rimmed bone china, linen napkins and crystal glasses made it the most elegant experience of her life.

"Something we actually agree on," he teased before forking another bite of cannoli into his mouth. His eyes lit up with excitement, and he swallowed before adding, "Hey, I'm going to be an uncle again."

Jessica felt a sharp tug in the vicinity of her heart. "That's wonderful. Congratulations. Sara?"

"Yep." His expression turned sheepish. "Although I wasn't supposed to tell anyone yet, so keep it to yourself, please."

"My lips are sealed." She returned her attention to her own dessert, a yummy dishful of chocolate gelato, but somehow she'd lost the rest of her appetite. Not that she needed any more food, she thought with a rueful smile. She'd already eaten enough to sustain her for two weeks.

"What's so funny?"

She looked up in surprise. "Huh? Oh, nothing. A touch of heartburn," she lied, her smile widening. She spooned some of the Italian ice cream into her mouth. Good, but not quite as good as the cannoli.

Garrett chuckled. He took a long swallow of his water, then set his glass down and said, "So, have you thought about having kids of your own?"

Jessica gulped back the gelato in surprise and choked.

Garrett shot up and came around to her side of the table. He patted her back as he handed her the water glass. "Are you all right?"

Nodding, she guzzled down the water and tried to convince herself the entire restaurant wasn't staring at her. When she felt like she could talk, she murmured, "I'm fine. I just wish the floor would open up and swallow me whole."

Garrett glared at the people at the next table who were openly gawking at her. He took his seat, clasped his hands and propped his elbows on the table. "That's the second time you've freaked out when I've mentioned kids. Granted, the first time I deserved what I got—"

"Jamison, I already told you, my personal life is off limits," she said in a low tone.

His expression hardened. "I thought we were past that nonsense. I thought we were getting to know each other better. Isn't that usually why people go out on dates?"

Tears burned her eyes, but she held his gaze. "You don't understand."

"Then explain it to me, Jessica, because I want to understand." He lowered his voice. "I'd like to get to know you, and I thought you felt the same."

She dabbed at her eyes with the napkin. "In another lifetime, I would have."

"What the hell does that mean, 'in another lifetime?' Dammit, woman, you're driving me crazy with all this secretive shit." He blew out a frustrated breath and swiped his fingers through his hair.

"I told you the other day I wasn't interested in anything other than," she cast a quick, furtive glance around her before adding in a whisper, "sex."

"Yeah, friends with benefits, I remember. But sweetheart, I know as much about you as I do the weatherman. If we're friends, shouldn't we at least know the bare minimum about each other? Hell, if I wanted to sleep with a stranger, I'd head to Krupp's and hook up with Mandy."

A stab of jealousy hit Jessica right between the eyes. "Who the hell is Mandy?" The words were out before she could stop them, and she could have kicked herself when a slow smile spread across his face. *Damn.*

"She's a bartender who's been hitting on me for months."

"So, why haven't you slept with her then?"

His eyes narrowed as if he were contemplating her question. "Beats me. She's beautiful, sexy...fun to be around."

Jessica sat up straight, insulted. "Are you insinuating I'm not fun to be around?"

"You're not exactly a barrel of monkeys tonight," he said with a shrug. He ran his finger through a glob of cinnamon-ricotta cream that was left on his plate. "Man, do I love cannoli. And these are the best I've had, hands down. I'll have to order a dozen to take home."

Jessica watched in anticipation as he stuck his finger in his mouth and sucked off the sweet filling. She gave herself a mental shake and cleared her throat. "So, seriously, why haven't you slept with Miss Beautiful, Sexy, and Fun To Be Around?"

He wiped his hands with his napkin before meeting her gaze. "Because she's not the one I want."

"Who *do* you want?"

"Don't play coy, Jess. You know who I want. And you want me, too. Don't deny it."

She swallowed. Deny it? All the man had to do was touch her and she melted like marshmallows in a cup of hot cocoa. Oh, she wanted him all right, no question about it. But she had a sinking feeling it would be impossible to keep from falling in love with this man. And love was something she wanted no part of. Along with love came commitment, marriage...children. Things she no longer had an interest in. Not now—maybe not ever.

"You're a hottie, Jamison," she stated matter-of-factly. "And you and I both know I'd be lying if I said I wasn't attracted to you, or that I didn't want you."

He looked thoroughly exasperated. "Then why the games? You pull me in, you push me away. It's damned frustrating."

Jessica glanced around the restaurant and noticed a few people were still eyeing them. "Please, can we just get out of here and talk about this later?"

Garrett nodded and motioned for the waiter.

He'd just unlocked the passenger-side door when he snapped his fingers with a muttered curse. "I forgot the cannoli. I'll be right back."

He started back across the parking lot as Jessica opened the door to climb inside. She heard the screech of tires and spun around just in time to see a large car speeding straight for Garrett.

Six

A scream tore from Jessica's throat; she stood frozen in fear. But the car swerved a split second before Garrett dove between two parked vehicles, as if the driver had a last minute change of heart. Then it sped out onto Military Avenue heading north.

She raced across the parking lot. "Garrett! Oh my God, are you all right?"

Garrett climbed to his feet and swore up a blue streak. "I couldn't make out the license plate number. Did you happen to catch it?"

Desperately afraid her knees were about to give out, she murmured, "No...I'm sorry, I didn't even think..."

He wrapped his arms around her, saving her from collapsing into a puddle on the asphalt. "Shhh, don't worry about it. Are you all right? Jesus, you're shaking."

She snuggled against his chest and took a deep, shuddering breath. "Y-you could've been killed. Who in the world would..." The words froze in Jessica's mouth.

My God...Wade? He *had* promised to come after her once he got out of prison, and the guy had a jealous streak a mile wide. Jessica hadn't been able to even look at another man without him going ballistic and starting a fight. But would he really try to run someone down? Her common sense said no. The idiot had just gotten out of prison. But then, who else? Jessica didn't believe in coincidences.

"Sweetheart, it's all right," Garrett assured her as he tightened his hold. "I'm fine, and so are you. That's all that matters. It was probably just some kids being stupid and blowing off steam." He started walking her back toward his truck.

She nodded, deathly afraid she knew exactly who was responsible for this. And it wasn't a carload of teenagers. Wade had promised to come for her when he got out of prison, and for the first time since she'd met him, Jessica was afraid he'd kept his word.

Garrett pulled his truck into the driveway and killed the engine. He leaned back and glanced over at Jessica, who stared out the passenger window, her brow creased as if deep in thought. She hadn't said a word on the ride home, and frankly, he was starting to worry. He wanted so badly to reach across the seat and take her in his arms.

"It's over, sweetheart, I promise. Come on, let me walk you to your door."

She nodded without looking at him. Garrett got out of the truck and came around to open her door. She climbed down, slowly, into his waiting arms. He couldn't remember the last time he'd felt this protective of anyone who wasn't a blood relative. Hell, until Jessica, the strongest emotion he'd ever felt over a woman had been intense lust. Not that he wasn't in lust with Jessica. It just seemed to be...*more* with her. Yeah, he wanted to sleep with her. But he also wanted to protect her, take care of her, comfort her, keep her safe.

Jesus, he was falling in love with her. The revelation hit him so hard he almost lost his balance.

They reached her front door, and Garrett kept his arm around her while she dug her keys out of her purse. He watched her fumble to unlock the door for a few seconds, then gently took them from her and opened it himself. He escorted her in, shut the door, and led her to the sofa.

"Are you going to be all right?" he asked, once she was seated. "Can I make you a cup of tea or something?"

Jessica kicked off her sandals and curled her legs beneath her, but wouldn't let go of his hand. She finally met his gaze and said, "No, just...stay. Please. I don't want to be alone."

Garrett dropped down onto the sofa and gathered her into his arms. He didn't want to make light of what had happened, but her reaction to the attempted hit-and-run seemed a little extreme. Especially since she was about the feistiest woman he'd ever known.

He smoothed her hair back and examined her face. Her eye makeup had run a bit, but other than that, she looked beautiful, if a little distracted.

"I'll stay, if you want me to. How 'bout I fix you that cup of tea?"

She cleared her throat. "That'd be great. Thanks."

He'd just dropped a tea bag in the cup when he heard the faint creak of springs. A moment later, she appeared in the doorway of the kitchen, her face taut with chagrin.

"I'm sorry. You must think I'm the biggest wimp in the universe."

He strode over and cupped her cheek. "Not even close. But I do think there's something you're not telling me. I'd half expected you to race after the car and pitch your sandal at it, not get all quiet on me."

She dismissed his words with a shrug. Dislodging his hand from her face, she walked over to the table and sat down. "You have quite an imagination, Jamison. Must be that cop's instinct."

Garrett inwardly flinched. What an ironic choice of words, he thought. Of course, she couldn't have known how that simple statement would affect him.

He grabbed the mug of tea he'd made for her and followed her to the table. "I didn't imagine your reaction, Jess."

"You were nearly run over by car right in front of me," she pointed out. "How was I supposed to react?" She grabbed a couple of napkins from the holder and started wiping the smudged mascara from beneath her eyes.

Garrett took a deep breath and let it out slowly. Well, the good news? Jessica seemed to be back to her normal biting self. The bad news—someone had attempted to run him down, and that same someone had to have followed them from home. The thought froze the blood in his veins. Not because he was concerned about himself, but Jessica.

He hadn't worried too much about it earlier when Mike mentioned it, but Carl Montgomery had been released from the hospital a few days ago and transferred to Green Bay Correctional. He knew the connection was doubtful since Montgomery was a slug with few friends. But it was certainly worth looking into.

He rose to his feet. "Since you seem to be feeling better, I think I'll head home." She looked up, eyes wide, so he quickly added, "Sweetheart, if you want me to stay, I will. It's completely up to you."

She thought about it for a moment. "No...no. I'll be fine, thanks." She offered him a wide, unconvincing smile. "I'm good. Really."

"Liar." Garrett knelt down next to her chair and grasped her hand. "I had a great time tonight."

A small smile curved her lips. "Me, too. Though it would've been better if you hadn't gone back for the damn cannoli."

He chuckled, brought her hand up for a kiss, then rose back up. He smiled down at her, amazed—and a little discomfited—to realize that even with makeup smudged under her eyes, she was the most beautiful woman he'd ever seen. "'Night, Jess. I'll give you a call in the morning." With one last comforting smile, he strode for the door.

"Garrett?"

He paused. "Yeah?"

"I don't want you to go."

He turned to face her. Christ, she was going to be the death of him. "Sweetheart, I think I need you to be more specific."

Jessica rose to her feet and crossed the kitchen to stand before him. She reached up and placed both hands on his chest. Garrett closed his eyes for a brief second, but when he opened them, she was still there, staring up at him, her invitation unmistakable. He let out a deep, ragged breath.

"I want you." She slipped her arms around him and pressed her lips against his shirt-clad chest. "In my bed." Tilting her head back, she gazed up. "Is that specific enough?"

Garrett became lost in those incredible eyes. "Are you sure?" he asked, even as he grasped her by the waist and pulled her flush against him.

In response, she reached between them and ran her palm up his iron-hard erection.

He growled low in his throat and swept her up into his arms.

By the time he kicked her bedroom door open, Jessica had his tie undone and half his shirt unbuttoned. He switched on the lamp that sat on her nightstand and pulled back the flowered comforter before lying her down. The heady fragrance of her perfume wreaked havoc on his senses as did the clean scent of her freshly laundered sheets.

She rose up on her elbows and smiled at him; a siren's smile, sexy and seductive. Garrett's groin tightened painfully. He took a deep breath and let it out slowly—which he seemed to do a lot in her presence. The last thing he wanted to do was take her roughly. And the way he felt right now, gentle wasn't an option. Plain and simple, he wanted to fuck her hard and fast. The thought scared the hell out of him. He'd never experienced this urgent need to be inside a woman before, to claim her as his own.

Her smile faltered. "Garrett? Are you all right?"

"I..." He cleared his throat. "I don't want to hurt you."

She blinked, then her lips settled into a teasing smile. "Well, that makes two of us. Maybe I should've said so earlier, but I'm not really into that kinky stuff."

He kicked off his shoes and sat down on the edge of the bed, trailing his hand up her calf, her thigh, stopping at the hem of her dress. "You know that's not what I meant. It's just..." He met her gaze. "I want you so bad I could burst into flame. And I'm...big. I'm afraid I'll flatten you like a pancake."

She tipped her head back and laughed, the tinkling sound soft and seductive. "Don't worry, big boy. I'm made of sturdier stuff than that."

Sexy witch. He ran a slow hand up the curve of her waist, over the outer swell of her breast until he reached her throat. Continuing on, he teased the tender flesh just below her ear before leaning in to replace his hand with his lips.

A sigh escaped her as she melted into him, tangling her fingers in his hair.

Garrett couldn't wait another second. He slanted his mouth across hers with hungry abandon, swallowing Jessica's gasp of surprise. She tasted like pure heaven; sweet and hot, just like the tea she'd drunk. She met the thrust of his tongue and tightened her hold on his hair, exciting him even more.

When she climbed onto his lap, Garrett nearly lost it. She straddled him, her dress hiked up to her hips. He cupped her backside with both hands and fell backwards onto the bed, pulling her with him.

Jessica tore her mouth from his and sat back up. She caught her bottom lip between her teeth as she ran her hands down his chest, slowly, until she reached the last few buttons that needed to be undone. She spread his shirt open and explored some more, stopping to tease each nipple, casting a quick, almost shy glance his way. Garrett closed his eyes with a sigh of contentment. It had been way too long since he'd felt a woman's touch.

And this woman had definitely been worth the wait.

With stunning clarity, he confirmed how dangerously close he was to falling in love with her.

He grasped her wrists to stop her sweet torture and looked at her, really looked at her. Her eyes were dark with desire, her cheeks flushed, her mouth slightly open. He watched, transfixed, as her tongue came out and moistened her top lip. She smiled. A shy, hesitant smile as if concerned something was wrong.

Garrett reached up and tucked a stray lock of hair behind her ear. "I've never wanted another woman as much as I want you," he said. "You've got me tied up in knots, lady."

"Yeah? I like the way that sounds. Let's see if I can make you unravel."

She draped herself across his chest and captured his lips. Garrett grasped her backside again, squeezing and kneading the soft globes, reveling in the perfection of her silky skin. She ground herself against him, and he nearly came in his pants. He wanted her so bad he was shaking with it.

Jessica kissed him with a ferocity he'd never known before. Those full, sensuous lips moved against his with hungry fervor, her hot tongue seeking and mating with his. Eager hands smoothed over his shoulders, his arms, his chest. She broke the kiss, gently caught his bottom lip between her teeth, then kissed his chin, his jaw, nuzzled his ear. It'd be a miracle if he didn't explode into a puff of smoke.

In one quick motion, Garrett had her flat on her back. The little minx smiled and ran the heel of her foot up the back of his thigh. She was so tiny her legs were wrapped around his waist, his throbbing erection trapped between himself and the bed. Jesus, he felt like a friggin' giant lying on top of her.

"Are you sure I'm not crushing you?" he whispered against her ear.

"I'm sure." She feathered kisses along his jawline. "I

love the feel of your weight on me."

Unconvinced, Garrett rolled to the side and propped his head on his hand. He traced her lower lip with his finger, then trailed a path down her chin, her throat, between her breasts. "I can't wait to see you naked."

"Then why am I still dressed?"

A punch of lust hit Garrett so hard he wanted to rip her dress off in one mighty yank. It was a nice little black number, though, and she'd probably brain him if he ruined it. So he slipped his hand beneath her and attempted to unzip it instead. Jessica leaned toward him to give him better access.

He had the dress unzipped and over her head in no time, and thought he might explode as his eyes feasted on her matching black strapless bra and panty set. Her full breasts were held in the silky tube of material by miracle alone, and his hands itched to strip away the lacy scrap covering her mound.

He leaned down and pressed his lips to the warm flesh just above her bellybutton. Jessica cupped the back of his head and arched against him with a wanton sigh of contentment.

Garrett worked his hands beneath her and unclasped her bra, then tugged it off and tossed it aside. Her beautiful milky white breasts fell free, those luscious pink nipples pebbled and begging to be touched. He leaned down and took one taut nipple into his mouth while his fingers found and tortured the other, rolling it between his thumb and forefinger.

Jessica whimpered, her neck arched, hands clenched in his hair.

He released her nipple with a loud suck and switched his assault to her other breast. Her movements grew urgent, and Garrett knew he was dangerously close to embarrassing himself. He twirled his tongue around her nipple one last time before releasing both breasts so he could sit up.

Gazing down at her, his breath caught in his throat. He'd never seen a sexier sight than Jessica spread out before him, breasts bare, nipples puckered and wet from his mouth. Naked, except for that tiny scrap of black lace.

He shrugged out of his shirt, then stood so he could remove his slacks, socks, and boxer-briefs, all while Jessica watched him through heavy-lidded eyes. His erection sprang free, and he chuckled when her eyes widened. He stretched back out on the bed beside her.

"Very impressive," she purred, her voice low and provocative. She wrapped her fingers around him and gave a less than gentle squeeze, nearly putting him through the roof.

Gritting his teeth, Garrett fell back onto the pillow and let her stroke his rigid flesh. He knew he couldn't let her explore for long or he'd come to a humiliating end—literally. But the word "stop" wouldn't form in his mouth. She leaned forward and tongued his nipple as her thumb rolled over the head of his cock. Garrett captured both her wrists with a silent curse and took a deep, shuddering breath. He guided her forward until she was astride his waist, his throbbing erection nestled against her backside, right between her sweet cheeks.

"Sorry, sweetheart, but I want to be inside you when I come."

Her answering smile was knowing and sexy as hell. "I'd prefer that myself. But Jamison," she splayed her hands over his stomach and lowered her voice to a whisper, "you'd better hurry up. I can't last much longer."

Well, hell, that did it. He'd be lucky to get two strokes in before the party was over. He worked his fingers under the scrap of black lace, wet with the proof of her desire, and tore it off her in one quick jerk.

Before she had time to complain, Garrett tossed it aside and used both thumbs to find the glistening nubbin beneath her folds. "I want you more than I've ever wanted anyone...anything," he said, his voice reverent and thick with desire. He stroked her with tiny circles, and a raw cry of pleasure escaped her as her head fell back on her shoulders. He was hard as stone and pulsing against her backside.

Meeting his gaze, Jessica lifted herself up, grabbed his hard shaft, and slowly lowered herself onto him. His teethed clenched, his breath held in anticipation as she took him inside her tight sheath with exquisite care, inch by torturous inch.

He reached up to cup both her breasts, stroking her nipples with thumbs still wet from her own dew. Their moans of pleasure mingled as they joined together.

It took every bit of self-control he possessed, but Garrett managed to lie still while she worked her way down. She hadn't quite taken him all in when she started to lift back up. Her eyes had been closed, but she opened them halfway, swallowed and let out a sob of frustration.

"I wanted to make this good for you," she admitted in an agonized whisper, "but I can't wait. I swear, I'm going to come any second."

"Jesus," he breathed, capturing her wrists. "I think my heart just stopped." He placed her hands on his chest and grasped her hips. "Ride me, Jessica," he demanded, his voice low and guttural.

Eyes closed, head hung low, she did as instructed. Using his chest as leverage, she moved slowly up and down his thick shaft. After no more than four strokes, her nails bit into his chest and she cried out his name, her hips moving in frantic rhythm. Garrett grasped her ass with both hands and drove inside her, hard and fast. His shout of release echoed off the walls as he experienced the most intense orgasm of his life.

Once their breathing slowed, Garrett wrapped his arms around her and rolled to his side, reaching for the comforter to cover them both. He'd never felt such peace and contentment as he did at that moment.

That's when he realized, for the first time ever, he'd forgotten to put on protection.

Garrett blew out a silent breath swiped his fingers through his hair. Truth be told, it may not have been a complete accident. Maybe on some subconscious level he wanted to get Jessica pregnant. He knew he wanted her in his life. And having a child together would certainly accomplish that.

He also knew it was wrong, and if a woman had ever tried to trap him in such a way, he'd have been out the door in a heartbeat. Yep, he was some kind of hypocrite all right. But he'd also never been more sure of anything in his life. He and Jessica belonged together.

He could only hope that after tonight, she'd come to the same conclusion.

Jack Sutton flew into the lot of the seedy Starlite motel and threw the old Buick LeSabre he'd bought just that morning into park. He beat the steering wheel as a round of curses poured from his mouth. Fuck, fuck, *fuck*! He rubbed his eyes, hard, with his thumb and forefinger, then dropped his head back against the headrest.

Dammit to hell. He'd had the bastard right in his sights! The bitterness and vengeance that had burned in his soul for seven long years should've been fuel enough for Jack to mow the sonofabitch down without a single twinge of regret. Only it hadn't. At the last second, as if the hand of God had given the wheel a mighty jerk, he'd swerved away with no time to spare.

Jamison deserved to suffer long and hard, just as Jack had suffered all those years, rotting in a prison cell for a crime he'd never have committed in a million years. The public defender hadn't given a rat's ass about a nineteen-year-old punk with a mile-long rap sheet for every crime under the sun. Except the one he'd been innocent of—cold-blooded murder.

With a sigh of disgust, he threw the car door open and climbed out. It took him almost a full minute to work the bent key into the lock of room number eight. Finally, with a hard twist, he shoved the door open. He'd left the lamp on because the distinctive scratch of cockroaches scurrying back into the woodwork every time he flipped on the light made his goddamn skin crawl.

Jack tossed his keys on the nightstand, then grabbed a can of cola out of the ice bucket and popped it open. He guzzled half it down, tore open a bag of cheese puffs, then turned on the television and made himself as comfortable as he could on the ratty, stained olive-green bedspread that was no doubt twice as old as he was.

Okay, so seven years behind bars hadn't turned him into the ruthless killer he'd suspected it would. When push came to shove, he'd no more been able to mow Jamison down than he'd been able to pop a cap into Eddie Morales, the drug dealer he'd been convicted of killing.

But as he'd fled from the restaurant, another idea had formulated in Jack's mind.

And this one would be so much more fun than the last.

Seven

Jessica nestled her tush into the warmth of Garrett's body with a smile so wide her jaw hurt. They'd made love, and it had been the most incredible experience of her life. He'd been gentle, but not too gentle, and her face grew warm as she recalled every kiss, every touch, every caress. He'd played her body like a finely tuned instrument, and even now, less than an hour later, she wanted him again.

As if the man could read her mind, he grew hard against her backside. "You awake?" he murmured in that deep, sexy voice, his hand cupping her breast, his fingers working her nipple into a tight bud.

"Like I could possible sleep through this."

Garrett abandoned her breast to run his hand down her belly, through the triangle of damp curls until his fingers found and gently spread open her wet folds. She moaned softly as he sank one finger into her slick passage, easing it in and out in a slow, steady rhythm. Her neck arched and her hips moved in beat with his finger. He used his thumb to stroke her swollen clitoris as he eased a second finger inside her. Jessica's breath hitched. She bit down on her bottom lip to keep from crying out.

"Lift your leg and drape it back over my thigh," he instructed, his breath warm against her ear. Jessica did so without question, the position opening her up to him. The distinct crinkle of a condom wrapper reached her ears seconds before his fingers were replaced by his hot, thick erection.

Jessica closed her eyes as he filled her, slowly and with care. Garrett Jamison was a giant in every sense of the word. She could barely accommodate him comfortably. She recalled that old saying about the size of a man's foot being in proportion with his manhood. Judging by the size of this man, there was no doubt in her mind the adage was true.

He grasped the top of her thigh as if to hold her steady while he slid himself in and out, slowly at first, entering her only a few inches at a time. But as their breathing became faster, so did his thrusts, and he sank himself deeper with each sweet stroke. Without warning, Garrett pulled out and laid her flat on her back. His face strained with need, he spread her thighs, captured her lips, and sank inside her to the hilt.

As their tongues and mouths mated with wild abandon, so did their bodies. No longer concerned with crushing her, Garrett made love to her as if it were their last day on earth. Jessica wrapped her legs around his waist and held on for dear life as he rode her hard and fast, their heated flesh slick with sweat.

They reached climax together. He tore his mouth free, pushed himself up and hung his head as they came in unison, their mingled raw cries of satisfaction filled the room. Garrett held himself up on his elbows, their hips still moving and straining as delicious little aftershocks rolled through her.

MEANT TO BE

"Jesus, am I still alive?" He murmured once their sated bodies lay in blissful numbness.

Jessica caressed his back with both hands and managed a shaky chuckle. "If your racing heartbeat's any indication, yep, you're still in the land of the living."

He struggled back to his elbows. "I'm sorry, I must be crushing you."

"Just a little," she admitted, letting out a monster yawn.

Garrett sat up and stretched his arms over his head, then climbed to his feet and headed for the master bathroom on wobbly legs. "Hell, woman, you wore me out," he teased as he stumbled inside and flipped on the light.

Jessica sat up and listened as he turned on the faucet and wondered if he was washing up because he planned to head home. Her heart sank at the thought. She'd wanted to sleep in his arms all night. Leaning against the headboard, she just hoped her disappointment didn't show on her face.

He turned off the light and returned to the bed, leaning over to flip on the lamp. "Hungry?"

She shook her head and pulled her legs up, wrapping her arms around them and resting her cheek on her knee. "I'm good. You can head home if you want."

"Are you kicking me out of bed? Damn, I feel so...cheap."

He grinned, and her lips twitched. "No, I want you to stay. I mean, if you want to." Good Lord, did that sound as pathetic to him as it did to her?

Garrett ran the pad of his thumb over her lips. "I want to," he assured her. "But I'm friggin' starving. Got anything to eat?"

Jessica smiled and climbed out of bed. Now that her good mood had returned, she slipped into the fuzzy powder-blue robe that hung on a hook behind her door and skipped toward the kitchen. Garrett followed her in a moment later. He'd pulled on his crumpled slacks but hadn't bothered to button them.

"So, what are we having?" he asked, taking a seat at the table and kicking his big feet up onto the chair directly across from him.

The man was so unbelievably handsome it nearly took her breath away. "Grilled ham and cheese sandwiches. And there's a bag of potato chips on the cupboard behind you."

He looked over his shoulder before leaning back to snag them off the shelf.

Jessica listened to him munch on chips as she gathered the bread and butter from the cupboard, and the ham and cheese singles from the fridge. Frankly, she was glad for the quiet. She just wanted to enjoy this little bit of domesticity. It had been so long since she'd truly enjoyed a man's company. And she didn't mean sex, although *that* had been unbelievable; beyond words. But just this comfortable companionship. It was nice. Something she'd truly missed over the last couple of years.

Oh, who the hell am I kidding, she thought, as she buttered the bread and assembled the sandwiches in the pan. Her relationship with Wade had been nothing but volatile from the moment they'd met. At sixteen, his brooding, bad boy act had been sexy as hell. After four years of living in a one-room efficiency apartment with barely enough money to keep the electricity on while he lay on his lazy ass all day, the thrill had definitely worn off.

"Those almost done?" Garrett asked, popping her back into the present.

She slid the grilled sandwiches onto plates and carried them to the table. Her mouth crooked at the sight of Mr. Louie sprawled across his lap getting the scratching of his life. Not that she had anything to feel jealous about anymore. Having experienced those magical hands herself, she could certainly relate to the loud purring and eyes closed in ecstasy. Garrett continued to scratch Mr. Louie while he wolfed down his two sandwiches, which made him an even better catch in her estimation.

Her hand halted halfway to her mouth. 'An even better catch?' What in God's name was she thinking? She didn't want a man in her life. And she didn't deserve a decent man like this one, not after the gazillion bad choices she'd made.

But he doesn't have to know about any of that, her heart argued back. *Your old life is a million miles away, and if he hasn't looked into your past by now, why would he?*

"Jess? Hey, you all right? You're starting to look a little green around the gills."

She set the sandwich down on her plate and got up to pour them each a glass of milk. "I'm fine. Just rethinking putting a greasy grilled sandwich in my stomach at," she glanced at the clock, "eleven o'clock at night. Probably should've just had a plain old ham and cheese on rye."

She wasn't sure whether he bought it or not, but he smiled as he wiped the crumbs from his hands and mouth.

"Well, they were tasty, so I'm glad I have an iron stomach. Sorry, boy," he said as he set Mr. Louie on the floor and rose to his feet.

Once they finished eating, Jessica carried their plates and glasses to the sink. When she turned back around, Garrett was waiting for her with an outstretched hand and a smile.

Pushing all thoughts of her loser ex-husband from her mind, Jessica slipped her hand into his and followed him back to the bedroom.

Incessant pounding on her back door woke Jessica up out of a sound sleep. She squinted her eyes against the early morning sun filtering in through the blinds and sat up with a jaw-popping yawn. Beside her, Garrett slept like the dead. With a shake of her head, she slipped out of bed.

After a quick glance at the clock, she shrugged into her robe and headed into the kitchen. When she pulled back the curtains and saw Ethan standing there, looking none too happy, a groan escaped her. What in the world were Mike and Sara thinking letting the little bugger roam the streets at seven o'clock in the morning?

Pasting a smile of welcome on her face, she swung open the door.

"Morning, Ethan. What can I do for you?"

He glared up at her. "Is Uncle Garrett here? We gotta finish building my dog house."

With a silent sigh, Jessica unlatched the screen door and let him inside. "Why don't you have a seat at the kitchen table, and I'll go get your uncle."

"Great, more freakin' banging," she grumbled as she stalked back into her bedroom. She stood beside the bed with her arms crossed, glaring down at the oblivious man. A reluctant smile lifted her lips when he rolled onto his side and reached for her, then patted the bed as if she'd somehow gotten lost in the comforter.

"I'm right here, Jamison. And I'd advise you get your lazy bones up and dressed. Ethan is sitting at my kitchen table waiting for you to come finish his dog house."

He sat up in a rush, eyes widened in comical dismay. "Shit, I completely forgot. Does he know I'm here?"

She rolled her eyes. "Uh, yeah, brainiac. Why do you think he's sitting in my kitchen looking like I stole his best friend?"

Garrett rubbed his face with both hands and muttered, "Jesus, someone's a grouch this morning."

She gathered his clothes from around the room and tossed them on the bed. "I'm in a great mood. Now get dressed and get the hell out."

He slipped into his slacks, then pulled on and buttoned his shirt. "Aren't you going to cook me breakfast?"

She let out a loud snort.

Laughing, he took her into his arms. "All right, grumpy goose. You climb back into bed. I'll take Ethan home and beg some breakfast from Sara. And I'll eat slow so you should get another hour of sleep before the hammering starts."

"Don't do me any favors," she groused against his chest. *Grumpy goose?* How could the man make her feel like a woman all night long, then within the space of a heartbeat, a five-year-old child?

"Come on, Uncle Garrett!" Ethan hollered from the kitchen. "You promised!"

Garrett kissed her on the top of the head and gave her

a quick swat on the backside. He strode out the door, his jacket and tie slung over his shoulder, whistling a merry tune. Jessica swung her foot at him, but all she did was stir the air. With a sigh of disappointment, she climbed back into bed and pulled the covers over her head.

By the time Jessica opened her eyes again it was just before nine o'clock. Hammering reached her ears, but it wasn't a steady pounding like last time. She sat up with a groan, deciding a pot of coffee was in order. Usually, she started the day with a cup of tea, but after the wonderfully exhausting night she'd had, a cup of tea just wouldn't do the job.

She tossed the covers back and slid from the bed, amazed to discover she was sorer than she'd been two hours ago. And she had to work second shift tonight, she remembered with another groan.

After putting on the coffee, she jumped in the shower, anxious for the steaming spray to ease her aching muscles. She closed her eyes, flattened her palms against the white tile, and let the hot water work its magic.

Twenty minutes later, she emerged from the bathroom feeling a hundred percent better. After slipping into her robe, she headed back into the kitchen for coffee and a couple slices of toast slathered with butter and strawberry jam, then carried everything into the living room.

She'd just picked up her second piece of toast when a special report interrupted her morning talk show. *Perfect opportunity to go top off my coffee*, she thought. She slapped the toast back down on her plate, grabbed her coffee mug and headed back into the kitchen.

Her breath caught as she gazed out the window and caught sight of a shirtless Garrett, hands propped on his hips, a huge smile transforming that handsome face as he gazed down at his nephew. Garrett threw back his head and laughed, as did Ethan, and Jessica's heart swelled. She was in love with the man. The truth hit her with such force she dropped her coffee cup into the sink.

"Dammit!" She took a deep breath and let it out slowly before chancing another look out the window. The sight of Garrett swinging a laughing Ethan around brought tears to her eyes, and it was all she could do to keep from bawling like a baby.

A sudden thought occurred to her, and she pressed a hand to her belly with a start. A thought she hadn't let her mind dwell on in the heat of the moment, but was hitting her like a slap of cold reality in the light of day. They hadn't used protection the first time—and she was smack dab in the middle of her cycle. A wave of dizziness overcame her. She staggered into the living room and collapsed onto the rocker-recliner.

Pregnant? The thought scared the living hell out of her. But Garrett was a wonderful man, and just from watching his interaction with his nephew she had no doubt he'd make a wonderful father—caring, loving, protective.

A much better father than her ex had turned out to be.

She massaged her throbbing temples and returned her attention to the television just as the special report wrapped up. A bus had been sideswiped by a moving van, then crashed into a telephone pole. No fatalities, thank God, but several people had been taken to the hospital with non-life threatening injuries. Jessica turned the TV off, leaned her head back, and closed her eyes.

Mr. Louie, as if sensing her inner turmoil, jumped up on her lap and made himself comfortable.

As she stroked his back, she couldn't help wondering what her life would be like if she was, in fact, pregnant with Garrett's child. Would he marry her? Did she even want to get married again? He could be a crabby SOB...but hey, so could she. They barely knew each other, yet sometimes when he looked at her, she felt like they'd known each forever. And they were certainly a perfect fit, as ridiculous as that seemed considering he was over a foot taller than her and outweighed her by at least a hundred and fifty pounds.

But, wow...she'd never felt more safe than when Garrett held her in his arms. The man was an incredible lover, too, although she'd keep that bit of news to herself since his head was big enough already. And he'd certainly come a long way with Mr. Louie, she acknowledged as she scratched behind the lazy fur ball's ears.

For the first time in a very long time Jessica considered the possibility that maybe a family was in the cards for her after all. Maybe God planned on giving her a second chance...

A second chance to do what, exactly? Her first shot at motherhood had ended in tragedy. One she'd barely recovered from. How could she even think about going down that road again?

Remembering she had laundry to do before her shift started, Jessica blew out a hard breath, set a disgruntled Mr. Louie on the floor, and headed down to the basement. She'd just finished folding the second load when the phone rang.

"Hello?"

"Hi, may I please speak to Jessica?"

"This is Jessica. Can I help you?"

"Jessica, this is Pam Harty, I'm a triage nurse at St. Mary's Hospital. I'm calling to inform you that your husband was in a bus accident today."

Eight

"You wanna run that by me again?" Assaulted by warring emotions, Jessica stumbled back until her heel collided with the sofa, and plopped down before her knees could give out.

"I realize this is a shock, but let me assure you your husband is going to be fine. He's suffered several contusions on his face and chest, and he broke both his left leg and left arm. He's pretty crabby, but considering all he's been through—"

"Are you talking about Wade? Wade Hastings? He was in that bus accident?"

"Yes. Mrs. Hastings, are you all right? Your husband can't be released from the hospital until someone arrives to drive him home, but frankly, it doesn't sound as if you're in any condition—"

"Here, let me talk to her," said the one voice she'd hoped to never hear again.

Jessica squeezed her eyes shut and prayed this was all some horrific joke.

"Hey, baby. You there?"

Nope, no joke, she thought, fighting to hold on to her composure. She'd never have believed God could be this cruel.

"Come on, Jessie, talk to me."

"How did you get my number?" she demanded, relieved to hear the confidence in her voice. "And what the hell are you doing in Green Bay?"

"Hey, darlin', can I get a little privacy here?" she heard him ask someone in that slithery voice she used to find so attractive. Then, "Jessie, can we talk about all that later? I really need you to come pick me up. They won't let me leave without a ride."

She couldn't believe her ears. After everything that'd happened, he actually expected her to come pick him up? She felt a hysterical urge to laugh only there wasn't a damn thing funny about any of this. "You must be out of your mind. I told you I never wanted to see you again, and I meant it!"

"Calm down." He lowered his voice. "Look, I know you don't owe me a damn thing, but I'm begging you, please, come pick me up. I've got a cast on my arm and on my leg, my head is bandaged up. Hell, I can't even take a piss on my own. Baby, I'm begging you. I'd get down on my hands and knees if I could."

Jessica closed her eyes and sucked in a deep breath. Why the hell was this happening? Just when her life had taken a turn for the better, the devil was trying to worm his way back in. Because of him, she'd been depressed for the better part of two years, unable to leave the house, crying herself to sleep almost every night. It wasn't until Uncle Charlie announced his plan to travel and offered her the use of his home that Jessica knew the time had come. Her grieving period had come to an end, and she'd needed to make a decision about her future. Marky would understand.

"Come on, baby, please. I need you."

Jessica shot to her feet and started pacing. "You call me baby one more time and I'm hanging up."

He had the nerve to chuckle. "I'll be good, I promise."

She stopped pacing and leaned against the wall, tipping her head back. "If I pick you up, where am I dropping you off?"

"I came all this way just to see you. I was hoping I could stay with you—"

"For-get it. No way in hell."

"Damn, Jessie, have a heart. I can barely fucking move." He paused, and she could hear his sigh of frustration. "I'm sorry, it's just...you know I don't do helpless well. You used to know me better than anyone."

Her lip quivered, and she hated herself for feeling even an ounce of compassion for the man. But she'd loved him so much at one time—at least, she'd thought it was love. And, luckily for him, it just wasn't in her to leave someone injured and helpless. Even Wade.

"It would only be for a week or two," he assured her. "Just until I'm mobile enough to travel back to Seattle. Please, Jessie. I won't be any trouble. You have my word."

She must be nuts to even consider picking this man up let alone allow him to stay in her home, even if it was for only a week. She must truly have lost her mind.

"I'll be there as soon as I can."

Jessica saw him as soon as she walked through the sliding double doors of the ER. He sat in a wheelchair looking incredibly bored, his broken leg in a full cast and propped up, his arm in a sling. A pair of crutches leaned against the wall beside him. His right cheek sported dark bruising, his right eye black and blue, but it didn't look nearly as bad as the nurse had made it sound.

"You look terrible," she lied, just to be ornery. Wade's good looks had always been more important to him than anything else.

"And you look even more beautiful than I remembered. I've missed you."

She cleared her throat and glanced around uncomfortably. "You never did tell me how you got my number. Or found out where I live."

He shrugged with his good shoulder and admitted, "My mom went into your parents' shop for a coffee and overheard them talking."

"That was sneaky," she said, truly hurt. "I've always thought better of your mother."

"Come on, you know my mom adores you. It's just, she thinks we belong together. So do I," he added, reaching out to caress her arm.

She snatched it away. "Well, you and your mother both need to face reality. You and I are through, Wade. I don't know what else I can say to make it any clearer."

He stared at her for a moment in quiet contemplation. "Look, I don't want to cause you any more pain than I already have. But I love you. I've loved you for so long, I don't know how to stop."

Tears burned the backs of her eyes. He sounded so sincere, she almost believed him...almost. But whether she believed him or not wasn't even relative anymore. She'd moved on with her life. It had taken almost two years, but she'd finally made peace with the past and looked forward to the future. A future that hopefully included Garrett Jamison.

Omigod, Garrett! In all the excitement, she'd completely forgotten to consider what he'd think about all this. Nothing good, that was for sure. She wondered if she could keep him out of her house for the next week or so, just until she could stick Wade on a bus back to Seattle. Yeah, fat chance of that happening. And hell, knowing Garrett, he'd probably insist on moving in with her as soon as she explained the situation to him. Talk about awkward.

"Let's just get out of here before I change my mind. Have you been discharged?"

"Yep." He waved to the woman sitting behind the triage desk. "All set. Mind grabbing my bag for me?" He pointed to an old, black duffle bag sitting on the chair beside him.

She snatched it up just as the woman approached and asked in a disgustingly cheerful tone, "Ready to go?"

Ever the charmer, Wade gave her his big, toothy smile. "That I am, darlin'."

The nurse grabbed his crutches and wheeled Wade outside. Once they had him seated in the front passenger side, she put the crutches in the back of the truck, told them to take care, and rolled the wheelchair back into the hospital.

They drove in silence for a while before Wade asked, "So why Wisconsin? I mean, I would've figured Vegas or L.A. Maybe even Chicago or New York. But cow country?"

She cast him a quick glance as she made a right onto Packerland Drive. "It was far away from you."

"Far away from Marky, too."

Her hands gripped the steering wheel with such force

her fingers went numb. "Don't you *dare* say his name," she gritted out. "Or I swear, I'll push you out of the truck right now."

"Look, I'm sorry, it's just...dammit, he was my son, too."

She swung a right into Walgreen's parking lot, came to a grinding halt, and threw the truck into park. "Get out."

"Jessie, I'm sor—"

She turned to face him, so angry she thought she might implode. "I said get out!"

He didn't budge, not that he could have anyway, she knew. He simply stared at her as if waiting for her to sprout horns and a tail. She blinked a few times, put the truck in drive, and pulled back out onto Packerland.

Wade wisely kept his mouth shut until they'd pulled into her uncle's driveway. She cast a quick glance next door and breathed a silent sigh of relief when she didn't see Garrett's truck parked out front. She wasn't in the mood to have that particular confrontation.

She helped Wade into the house, praying all the while none of the Jamisons were home to witness it. Once she had him settled on her couch, she handed him the remote and said, "I need to get ready for work."

"Work?" he repeated, his tone incredulous. "But what the hell am I supposed to do? I don't even know if I can hobble to the bathroom on my own."

She walked into the kitchen, opened the cabinet below the sink and pulled out an empty milk jug. She walked back into the living room and tossed it to him. "If you have to go, stick it in here. And let's get a few things straight right now. If the phone rings, let the machine get it. If someone comes to the door, don't answer it. And if you eat the last chocolate cupcake, don't be here when I get home."

As soon as Jessica walked out the front door, Wade leaned down and fished through his duffle bag for his cell phone. He dialed his mother's number as he watched Jessica's truck back out of the driveway.

"Hello?"

"Hey, it's me."

"Wade, thank God!" his mother cried into the phone, nearly busting his eardrum. "I could wring your neck for worrying me like this. Why didn't you call?"

He leaned back against the couch's armrest and closed his eyes. "If you promise not to scream in my ear again, I'll tell you what happened."

"Should I sit for this?" she asked.

Wade told her about the bus accident and everything that had happened since.

"This is crazy, Wade. You can't stay there alone while Jessie's at work. I'll hop on a plane and come take care of you myself—"

"Don't be ridiculous," he said. "You can't afford to take time off work right now with Lyle's stupid ass getting fired. You'll never make the mortgage."

"Then come home. Your brother can take care of you while I'm at work."

"I can't very well win Jessie back if I'm in Seattle," he pointed out, squeezing the bridge of his nose. His mother didn't need to know the real reason he'd come after Jessica. "Besides, I have a better idea. Put Lyle on the phone."

Declining to work overtime for the first time since he'd gotten hired nearly twenty years ago, Luke Jamison whistled as he made his way to the parking lot.

He planned to pick up flowers and a bottle of wine on his way home, then get in a quick shower before heading over to Muriel's place.

Muriel stood on her front porch watering a hanging basket of red petunias when he arrived. She waved as soon as she saw him. "Right on time," she said as she stepped off the porch to meet him.

Luke smiled and handed her the bottle of wine. Her brows lifted when she read the label. "Well, this'll certainly go down a lot smoother than the bottle of cheap stuff I picked up."

Luke chuckled, feeling a little more relaxed with each passing moment. He held out his other hand, and the look of delight on Muriel's face made it worth every penny.

"Tulips! But how did you—"

"Garrett told me tulips are your favorite flower."

Clutching both the pricey bottle of wine and paper-wrapped bouquet to her chest, Muriel gazed up at him as if he'd just handed her a star and a moonbeam. "I hope you didn't go to too much trouble. Tulips are pretty much out of season."

"It was no trouble at all. They had them at the first place I stopped." The third, actually, but Luke would've driven all over Green Bay if he'd had to.

She smiled a moment longer before saying, "Well, my goodness, you didn't come over just to stare at my front porch. Come on in. You can open the wine while I set the table."

He followed her into the house through the back door, which opened up right into her spacious kitchen. After setting the bottle of wine on the counter, she dug a corkscrew out of a drawer, and pulled two wine glasses from the cupboard. While he made quick use of the corkscrew, she grabbed a clear glass vase out from under the sink, filled it halfway with water, and lovingly arranged the tulips.

"Dinner smells wonderful," he said. "I want to thank you again for making the pierogies. I know they're a lot of work."

"I'll let you in on a little secret. I made them about a month ago. They freeze well, and all my kids love them, so I make a big batch every few months." She slid the sautéed pierogies onto the platter around the pork roast and carried it to the table.

Luke set the wineglasses on the table. "Is there anything else I can help you with?"

"Nope. You just plant yourself in that chair and relax."

With a huge smile of contentment, Luke sat. He still couldn't believe he was in Muriel's home, about to eat a meal she'd prepared especially for him. For the first time in a very long time, he felt special.

Muriel set a steaming bowl of sauerkraut on the table, and his mouth started to water.

"I didn't boil any potatoes because the pierogies are potato and cheese," she explained as she set a bowl of creamy cucumber salad in front of him. She took her seat and smiled across the table, her eyes glowing with something akin to adoration.

With the serving spoon for the sauerkraut held in mid-air, Luke smiled back.

They ate in silence for a good ten minutes before Muriel found her voice. "I hope you're enjoying the meal. I know you're used to eating well, with Sara being such a fantastic cook and all, but maybe this will come in a close second."

She gazed at him across the rim of her wineglass. Jeez, this was ridiculous. She felt like a schoolgirl out on her first date. Why, her palms were even sweaty!

"I swear, if you tell her I said this, I'll deny it with my dying breath, but this is the best meal I've ever had. And I mean ever." Luke backed up his statement when he tore into another potato and cheese-filled pocket with a hearty, "Mmmm."

Muriel laughed softly. "Well, whether that's true or not, it's the nicest compliment I've ever gotten."

"As beautiful as you are, I find that hard to believe."

Luke continued to eat his meal as if he hadn't just paid her the queen of all compliments. Her face heated with pleasure. She took another sip of her wine and continued to pick at her food.

He glanced up, frowning. "Is something wrong? You've hardly eaten anything."

"Oh, no, everything is fine. I had a late lunch and guess I'm not as hungry as I thought I'd be. But please, eat to your heart's content."

"Hell, I already have," he said, patting his belly. "I can't remember the last time I ate so much. Everything was delicious. Thank you."

"It was my pleasure." She cleared her throat and added, "Why don't we take the rest of the wine into the living room and watch a movie. By the time it's over, maybe we'll both have room for dessert."

"Sounds good. But first, can I help you clean up?"

Muriel thought she might swoon. *Man, if he's good in bed, I'm dragging his ass to the nearest preacher.*

"Thanks, Luke, but it'll only take me a few minutes to put the food away and the dishes in the dishwasher. Why don't you take our glasses and the rest of the wine into the living room and browse through my movies, see if there's something you might like to watch."

"Will do."

He met her gaze in an almost confident manner—which was odd considering he usually turned a light shade of pink whenever their eyes met. Muriel licked her lips in anticipation. Maybe he was finally coming out of his shell.

Or maybe the two glasses of wine he'd consumed were warming more than his blood.

Luke had just pulled a movie from her DVD cabinet when she joined him. "Excellent choice," she said as he handed her the case. She popped it in the Blu-ray player and curled up on the couch before patting the seat beside her.

He picked up his wine and sat stiff as a board with the glass clutched between his hands. So much for coming out of his shell. Muriel's lips pursed as she considered how best to loosen this shy man up.

"More wine?" she asked, pouring without waiting for a response.

Luke cleared his throat. "Thanks."

Very deliberately, Muriel turned so that her bare feet were resting against Luke's outer thigh. She saw him swallow, and a smile of satisfaction curved her lips.

She could simply jump him. Have him flat on his back before he knew what was happening. But the poor guy would probably die of a heart attack if she were to do something so bold. Good Lord, though, a woman could grow old waiting for man like this to make the first move. What to do, what to do...

"I was amazed to find this movie in your collection," Luke said, surprising her out of her reverie.

Leaning forward to grab her wineglass, Muriel not so accidentally brushed her breast against his forearm. "Oh, I love *The Changeling*. Without a doubt, my all-time favorite scary movie."

He glanced at her, brows slightly raised. "Mine, too. *Halloween* runs a close second. *The Shining* is another favorite of mine."

Excited to finally have a topic of discussion she could keep him interested in, Muriel said, "I have both those on DVD. Maybe I can cook you supper again sometime and we can watch one of them."

"Sounds good to me."

Muriel realized she had his full attention. She wasn't sure if it was the wine or not, but Luke looked very much like he wanted to kiss her. She set her wineglass down.

Yes, Virginia, there is a Santa Claus!

"Muriel?"

"Yes?"

"I, uh-I was wondering if, uh—"

She hiked her leg over his lap and straddled him. "Yes, you may," she said before wrapping her arms around his neck and slanting her mouth across his.

Luke sat motionless for a stunned second. Then he growled low in his throat and curled his big hands around her waist, pulling her tight against him.

Muriel smiled against his lips.

He pulled back slightly and whispered, "What's so funny?"

"I was just thinking about a conversation I had with Garrett."

Luke pinched her bottom, shocking and delighting her at the same time. "I am *not* gay."

"Oh, that stinker! I didn't think he'd tell!"

The phone rang. *Aw, come on. It was just getting good.* Muriel reached over and snatched the cordless off the end table. "Hello? Oh, hi, sweetie. Tonight?" She glanced at Luke with a pout of regret. "Sure...I know you can't help it. You can't afford to call in this soon...All right, see you in a few."

She disconnected the call and set the phone back on the table. "Well, it looks like we're going to have to continue this another night. My daughter just started a new job, and they asked her to come in tonight to fill in for someone. I have to watch my granddaughter, and she'll be sleeping over. This was the first time I've had the house to myself in months, too," Muriel muttered, eyeing his sexy lips with disappointment. "My younger three are spending the weekend at their father's."

Reaching up to cup her face in his hands, Luke pulled her down for a quick kiss. Eyes twinkling, he said, "You know, I just love cabbage rolls, but Sara rarely makes them since I'm the only one who'll eat them. And now that she and Ethan have moved in with Mike, we get so few home-cooked meals."

Muriel shivered with understanding. "Then you're in luck, because cabbage rolls happen to be another of my specialties. And I cook them in the pressure cooker so the cabbage practically melts off the meat."

Luke cleared his throat as his hands dropped down to her waist. "Do you use tomato soup or tomato sauce?"

Muriel stared at his lips as she replied, "Tomato soup.

With a few squirts of ketchup mixed in for a little tang."

"Good God, I think I love you."

Her laughter filled the room. "Ah, Luke, I really do hate to cut the night short. Promise me we'll do this again *soon*."

"Tomorrow night soon enough?"

NINE

Garrett pulled into the parking lot of the restaurant and killed the engine. He knew Jessica was working second shift tonight, and since Uncle Luke had a dinner date with Muriel, and Nicky planned to eat with Mike and Sara, Garrett decided to forego the usual pizza for one of the 'best burgers in town.'

He strode through the door and stood in line behind two couples and a family of five. The place was packed, and it took nearly fifteen minutes for him to be seated. He'd watched Jessica hustle back and forth so many times his head was spinning. And she looked tired, which annoyed him. He hated that she had to work so hard. Hated that she planned to work a second, part-time job just to make ends meet.

She finally approached his table, her smile oddly hesitant.

"Hey, sweetheart, any chance you could take a break and keep me company while I have supper?"

"Well," she cast a quick glance over her shoulder toward the back room. "It's pretty busy, and my boss is still here. But I can probably take my fifteen minute break soon." She pulled out her tablet and pen. "What would you like to eat?"

He winked at her. "You."

Her cheeks pinkened just the tiniest bit. "Seriously."

"I *am* serious. But for now, I'll take a double cheeseburger, fries, and a chocolate shake."

Jessica left to place his order and returned five minutes later with a large chocolate shake, piled high with whipped cream, and a soda for herself. She set them down and slid in across from him. Without making eye contact, she propped her elbows on the table and played with her straw.

Garrett took a sip of his shake, then used the straw to scoop some whipped cream into his mouth. "Good stuff. Maybe I should stop at the grocery store for a can on the way home. I bet whipped cream tastes even better on you than it does this shake."

She smiled, but it didn't quite reach her eyes.

He pushed his glass away and raked his fingers through his hair. "All right, spill."

"What?"

He sighed and leaned back in the booth. "Are you upset with me for not calling earlier? I meant to, but after finishing the doghouse, Ethan talked me into taking a ride to the arcade. And I kind of figured you needed a break from me anyway."

"I'm not upset with you. I just..." Her words trailed off as her gaze shifted awkwardly around the restaurant. Almost as if she felt guilty about something. She tucked a stray lock of hair behind her ear and said, "I'd better go check on your food."

Before he could stop her, she shot to her feet and headed for the kitchen.

Frustrated, Garrett laid his arm across the back of the booth and stared after her. What in the world had her acting so skittish? Did she regret their night together? The thought caused an uncomfortable ache in the middle of his chest. Christ, he was half in love with her, and if he didn't know any better, he'd swear she was about to give him the boot. But it didn't make a lick of sense. He knew she'd enjoyed their lovemaking every bit as much as he had. She couldn't be *that* great of an actress...could she?

Jessica stood by the pick-up window, chatting with one of the other waitresses, clearly avoiding him while she waited for his order. She cast a quick glance his way, grabbed a bottle of ketchup off the shelf beside her and picked up the steaming plate the cook had just set under the heat lamp. She didn't make eye contact with him as she approached the table, but her tone was light when she set his food and the bottle of ketchup down in front of him.

"Here you go. I even told the cook to throw on an extra slice of cheese for you."

Garrett didn't acknowledge her gesture or touch his food. He just watched her, waiting with bated breath for the words he was sure were coming. But she merely slid back onto the seat and surprised him by snatching one of the fries off his plate.

"Jamison, these things really are much better if eaten hot," she teased with a small grin.

"Are you PMSing or something?" He knew he risked having a drink dumped on his head by the chauvinistic question, but didn't care. "Because you've been acting strange as hell since I got here."

She scowled, eyeballed his chocolate shake, but must have thought better of it. It was quite doubtful he'd be able to save her job a second time, and he suspected she'd quickly come to the same conclusion.

"I've got a lot on my mind, you ass. Not to mention, it's been busy as hell, my feet are killing me, and I've already been informed I have to work a ten-hour shift instead of eight."

Good going, asshole. He reached across the table to grasp her hand, but she pulled it out of his reach with a 'don't touch me' glare.

"Look, I'm sorry. I can be an idiot sometimes, in case you haven't noticed." She snorted, and he couldn't help but grin. "Forgive me and I'll let you have another fry...?"

Looking at least slightly mollified, she snatched another fry off his plate with a muttered, "Whatever."

Deciding not to push his luck, Garrett ate his cheeseburger in silence, happy to just be in her company. Jesus, he thought as he sucked down a good third of his milkshake to mask his reaction, when had he become so attached? This growing need to simply be in her presence was really starting to scare the shit out of him.

"I won't get home 'til after midnight," she said as she stole another fry off his plate. She cast him a surreptitious glance through her lashes before adding, "And I'll be pretty tired...just so you know."

Garrett watched her through narrowed eyes as she took a sip of her soda, glancing everywhere and at everyone but him. He'd already come to the conclusion that his detective skills were lacking, but it didn't take Sherlock Holmes to figure out something was going on here. She as much as said she didn't want him stopping by tonight.

He stuffed the last bite of his cheeseburger into his mouth and washed it down with the rest of his milkshake.

After swiping a napkin across his mouth, he replied, "Don't worry, honey, I can take a hint."

"Garrett—"

He held up a hand. "You don't need to explain, I get it. You're tired." He smiled. "Hell, so am I." He stood up, pulled a twenty from his pocket and tossed it on the table. "Don't work too hard," he said. Then he turned and strode out the door.

Tears burned Jessica's eyes as she watched Garrett walk out of the restaurant; maybe out of her life. She'd wanted to tell him about Wade in the worst way, but every time she'd tried to form the words, she'd chickened out. She didn't know him well enough to predict what he might do, and that scared the hell out of her. And, of course, she'd made things worse by keeping quiet. The man was a cop after all. It didn't take him long to realize something was wrong.

And he was on a leave of absence from the force, which meant it would be impossible to keep him from finding out about her unwanted houseguest. Not that she wanted to keep secrets from him.

With a heavy heart, she cleared the table and paid his check.

By the time midnight rolled around, Jessica felt as if she'd worked a double shift instead of just a couple extra hours. Her feet were sore, she had a killer headache. Time had dragged at a snail's pace, and all she'd been able to do was dwell on the look on Garrett's face right before he'd walked out.

After mumbling a few quick goodnights, she grabbed her purse and headed home.

As she pulled up in front of her house, she couldn't miss Garrett's truck sitting in his driveway. Hell, she wasn't ready to face him, and she certainly didn't want to have to deal with Wade either. Unfortunately, the latter couldn't be avoided. Deciding to explain everything to Garrett tomorrow, she slid from her truck and hurried up the driveway. He'd have had a chance to cool down, and she'd have a chance to make other arrangements for her unwelcome ex. Maybe his mother could hop on a plane and escort his useless ass back home to Seattle with her.

Mr. Louie met her by the back door with a hearty, "Mrow!" Jessica scooped him up and carried him into the house.

As soon as she flipped on the kitchen light, Wade called out, "Jessie, is that you? I'm fuckin' starving here. Did you bring me something to eat?"

She set Mr. Louie down and tossed her purse onto the kitchen table. "Quit whining," she snapped as she stormed into the living room. She came to a grinding halt at the sight of him. He reclined back on the couch, one knee up, his broken leg propped on a pillow. His good arm tucked behind his head while his broken one rested on his chest. And all he wore was a pair of gray boxer-briefs.

Wade was a good-looking man and he knew it. He had a nice physique, lean and muscular with a fine mat of golden chest hair that tapered down his hard, flat stomach and disappeared into the waistband of his briefs. Hair a few shades darker than her own curled up around the nape of his neck while arrogant brown eyes stared back at her in knowing contemplation.

At one time, the sight of Wade lying on the couch in only a pair of briefs and a smile would have been an incredible turn-on. Now, it just left her cold.

"Sorry, baby, you know how cranky I get when I'm

hungry."

She stalked past him and yanked the drapes closed. "I told you not to call me baby. And how the hell did you manage to undress yourself?"

He reached out and grasped her arm. Before she realized his intentions, she found herself sprawled across his chest. He held her pinned against him, and her skin nearly crawled off her body when she felt the proof of his interest growing beneath her belly.

"Come on, Jessie. You want it just as much as ! do, admit it," he whispered in her ear, following his words with his tongue.

"Who the *fuck* is he?"

Jessica's head shot up with a squeal. "Garrett!"

He strode from the kitchen into the living room and stopped a couple of feet in front of the couch. "At least you remember my name."

His gaze hard and cruel, his lip curled with disdain, this was the Garrett she hadn't seen in almost two weeks. The Garrett she'd hoped never to see again.

Jessica slid off Wade and climbed to her feet. "This isn't what it looks like, you have to believe me."

She followed his line of vision and could have cried when she realized where his gaze had landed—on the very obvious erection straining Wade's boxer-briefs. And Wade, the bastard, had a smirk on his face the size of the Grand Canyon.

Garrett looked back at her, and she inwardly flinched at the disgust seething in his eyes.

"I know you think I'm a real dumbshit, but even a moron could connect the dots on this one."

"Hey, Paul Bunyan, why don't you go back out the way you came, and don't forget to lock the door. Jessie and I have unfinished bus—"

"You're dead!" Garrett snarled through his teeth. He pounced with the speed of a rattler, clipping Jessica in the process and sending her flying into the recliner. Wade screamed as Garrett's massive frame landed on top of him and his broken arm.

Jessica jumped to her feet and onto Garrett's back. She wrapped her arms around him and tried with all her might to wrest his forearm from Wade's throat. But her efforts were futile, and she sobbed as Wade's eye's rolled back into his head and his face turned purple. Choking sounds gurgled in his throat as spittle shot from his mouth.

"Garrett, please!" she cried, clawing at his hands. "You're going to kill him!"

All at once, he released Wade's throat and shot to his feet. Jessica fell backward onto the couch, but quickly scrambled back up to make sure Wade was still breathing. He wheezed and coughed, half curled into a ball.

"He ain't worth it. *You* ain't worth it," Garrett told her, his tone pure ice.

Jessica swore she could feel her heart being torn in half. "If you'd calm down and let me explain—"

"Believe it or not, honey, I don't need it explained to me. Thanks for the ride." With that parting shot, Garrett spun around and stormed out. She flinched when the back door slammed shut.

Wade's coughing spasms lessened enough for him to choke out, "I'm pressing charges! That sonofabitch is gonna pay for this!"

Jessica's breath caught. The last thing Garrett needed was an assault charge. She'd never forgive herself if he lost his badge because of her. She helped Wade to a sitting position, then ran into the kitchen for a glass of water.

"Just let it go," she advised when she returned. "He had every right to be pissed off."

Wade gulped down the entire glass, heaved a few more ragged breaths and collapsed back down on the couch. "Why? 'Cause he's boning you?" She opened her mouth and he hurriedly added, "Don't even waste your breath denying it. A man don't get that twisted up over a friend."

She snatched the glass from his hand, returned it to the kitchen, and stormed back into the living room. "It's none of your business what I do, or who I do it with," she informed him.

Jessica wanted to scream, she wanted to cry—she wanted to break Wade's good arm and leg with her bare hands. After more than two years of merely existing, she'd finally gotten her life back on track. She had a home, a job, a few friends. A lover. A wonderful, sexy, considerate lover...

Tears burned her eyes.

"You're damn right it's my business. You're my wife."

"*Ex*-wife!"

"I ain't screwing around, Jessie, I'm pressing charges. That bastard's spending the night in a jail cell."

He managed to climb to his feet, but when he reached for his crutches she hurried forward and snatched them out of his reach.

"Dammit, Wade, you are *not* pressing charges. If you'd have kept your big mouth shut, he wouldn't have jumped you. It's your own fault."

He used his good arm to hold himself up. "My fault? Are you kidding me? I'm laying here in an arm and full leg cast! That bastard jumped a defenseless man and he's gonna pay. Now you can either hand me the phone, or I'll crawl to it. But one way or another, I'm pressing charges."

The tears burning her eyes finally escaped, falling down her cheeks in hot streams. "Wade, please, if I ever meant anything to you, you'll let it go."

He stared at her, hard, his steely eyes boring into hers, his displeasure so palpable she could feel the heat of it from where she stood.

"Are you in love with him?" he asked, his voice menacingly soft.

Y*es!* "Of course not. I barely know him." She angrily swiped at her tears.

His gaze continued to bore into hers as he lowered himself back down on the couch. "Then why are you making such a big goddamn deal about it? I know you, Jess. You don't shed tears over someone you don't give a shit about."

"I told you, he means nothing to me," she insisted as she leaned his crutches against the wall. "We were seeing each other, but it wasn't serious. Maybe he thought there was more to it, I don't know. But I don't want to cause him any trouble, Wade, and I mean it."

"Promise me you won't see him again, and I'll think about it."

The thought alone caused her throat to swell up so thick she could barely swallow. Dammit, why did Wade have to come looking for her? Why couldn't he have just stayed on the west coast and left her the hell alone? He'd already taken so much from her it wasn't fair. It just wasn't fair.

But he had her over a barrel and he knew it, the bastard. Though he was right about that; he knew her better than just about anyone. And she'd thought she knew him, too.

"Get real. You really think he'd call me again after tonight?" Jessica scoffed. Inside she was dying. She could only hope that once Wade left, Garrett would give her a chance to explain.

Garrett slammed the front door closed behind him and stalked through the living room into the kitchen. He yanked open the fridge and grabbed himself a beer. His hands shaking with restrained rage, he drained half of it in one, long pull, then set the bottle down with more force than necessary. Hands braced on the edge of the counter, he hung his head in shame.

Jesus, he was possibly the biggest schmuck in the world. She'd told him, more than once, that she didn't want anything from him but sex. And like a complete idiot, he'd fallen for her. Not only that, he'd imagined having kids with the fickle bitch. A bitter, self-deprecating laugh burst from his mouth. Hell, she was probably laughing her head off right now. She and that smarmy prick she'd been ready to mount when Garrett walked in.

He snatched up his beer and drained the rest in another long pull.

Uncle Luke came up from the basement and padded barefoot into the kitchen. He set a glass in the sink before glancing over at Garrett and frowning. "Son, you don't look so good. Want to talk about it?"

"No." Garrett tossed the empty bottle in the recycling bin and grabbed himself another.

"You and Jessica fighting already?"

Garrett cracked it open and tilted the bottle to his lips. After a couple of gulps, he said, "What part of 'no' don't you understand?"

Undaunted, Uncle Luke leaned back against the sink and crossed his arms over his chest. "Whatever it is, you'll feel better after a good night's sleep."

Without sparing his well-meaning uncle a glance, Garrett polished off the rest of beer number two, grabbed his keys off the counter and strode toward the front door. "I'm going out."

"Garrett, I don't want you driving anywhere in your—"

"I'll be fine. Don't worry about it." He stormed out, climbed in his truck, and sped off down the road.

Ten minutes later he pulled into Krupp's parking lot and swung into his usual spot by the side door. Needing a minute, he swiped his fingers through his hair and leaned his head back against the headrest. Christ, he felt like the biggest damn loser in all of Wisconsin. Maybe after a couple more beers and a game or two of pool he'd wind down enough to head home and get some sleep. But right now, he needed to get his temper under control and settle the hell down.

As he approached the bar, the cloying scent of one too many perfumes mingled with a thick cloud of cigarette smoke, nearly choking him. Garrett wrinkled his nose as he dug in his wallet for a twenty.

"Hey, gorgeous, didn't expect to see you tonight."

Garrett slapped the bill on the bar and attempted a

smile. "Hey, Mandy. I'll take a bottle of Bud and five bucks-worth of quarters for the table."

Mandy gave him a considering look as she cracked open his beer. "You feeling all right?" she asked as she set the bottle in front of him. She slid the twenty off the bar and walked over to the register. When she returned, she set his change on a paper coaster, then propped her elbows on the edge of the bar, leaning forward to give him a great cleavage shot.

Garrett tilted the bottle back and took a healthy pull off it. He eyed the view she offered, moved his gaze upward and couldn't hold back a smile as she did the whole lick her lips thing. Mandy had been flirting with him for so long he didn't even pay attention to it anymore. She was pretty enough, he supposed, and certainly had a great rack. But for whatever reason he'd never felt enough of an interest to pursue her. He'd been called a lot of things, but no one had ever accused him of taking advantage of a woman.

"I'm good. Just need to blow off a little steam." He slid his change off the bar. "I'm sure I'll need another beer in about ten minutes, if you don't mind."

She tossed her shoulder-length, auburn hair and treated him to her perfected come-hither smile. "For you, anything."

Garrett shook his head, grabbed his beer, and headed for one of the open pool tables. As he pushed his quarters into the machine, he glanced up at the Budweiser clock that hung above the jukebox; five-after-one. Hell, later than he'd thought, and it explained why the place was nearly empty. Only a dozen or so people still hung around. A couple of guys sat at the far end of the bar watching a small group of women dance to some country tune about riding cowboys. Three booths were occupied—a loner sat nursing a beer at one, and the other two held several young couples chatting and laughing with each other.

After another pull off his beer, Garrett racked the balls, chose a cue stick, and broke.

He'd just cleared the table when Mandy approached with the second beer he'd requested.

"Here you go." She leaned back against the pool table and braced her arms behind her so that her best assets were once again on display.

Before he could thank her, a woman's muffled scream reached him from the far corner of the bar. Garrett threw the cue stick down and rushed over, furious to discover some piece of shit had one of the girls who'd been dancing pinned against the wall, his hand fumbling under her skirt, the other clamped over her mouth.

He grabbed the bastard by the mullet and tore him off the hysterical young woman. His anger hit full-boil as he watched her slide down the wall and curl up in a ball. Her two sobbing friends dropped to the floor and gathered her in their arms.

Garrett cracked the guy's head against the corner of the jukebox, then let go of his hair and grabbed the front of his shirt in one fist. He held him up so he could look him in the eye, literally lifting him off the ground. "What kind of a scumbag forces himself on a woman?" He backhanded the guy, feeling a rush of adrenaline so strong his whole body shook. "Someone needs to teach you that no means no."

"I-I was just givin' the tease what she was askin' for!" the moron sputtered as blood trickled from his busted lip.

One of the woman's friends swung her head around

and cried, "Liar! She told you to stay away from her, but you wouldn't listen!"

Red exploded behind Garrett's eyes. He held the guy up and swung, hitting him square in the jaw. Suddenly, an arm wrapped around Garrett's throat and another around his chest. The power behind those arms surprised him as he was yanked back. *Who the fu—?*

"Garrett, let him go!" a familiar male voice shouted in his ear. "You're about ten seconds away from killing the little prick, and I don't want to have to tell Sara you're in jail for murder. Come on, man, he ain't worth it. Let him go!"

Mike? Garrett squeezed his eyes shut and went still. Jesus, Sara was pregnant. This kind of stress could put her in the hospital. He opened his fist and let the bastard drop to the floor; he lay still as death.

Mike let Garrett go with a shove, walked around and nudged the guy with the toe of his boot. He curled up in the fetal position and let out a low groan.

"Well, he won't be able to blow his nose for a while, but he'll live." Mike pulled out his cuffs and shot Garrett a dark look. "Thank God Luke called me when he did. What the hell were you thinking?"

He couldn't believe his eyes. "You're going to arrest me? That scumsucker was about to rape—"

"Christ, use your brain. These aren't for you." Mike glanced around at the sea of faces gathered about and announced, "All right, show's over. Krupp's is officially closed for the night. Everybody pay your tabs and get on home."

Mandy, who dabbed at her eyes as if she'd been crying, ran up and threw her arms around Garrett's waist. "Are you all right? I was so worried."

He rolled his eyes as he patted her on the back. "I'm fine. Weren't you watching? I won."

She leaned back and smiled up at him. "You're a hero."

Garrett shrugged. "I just did what anyone would do."

Mandy gave him one last squeeze then walked off to talk to the owner.

Mike cuffed the guy and hauled him to his feet. The three young women promised to come down to the station in the morning to give their statements. Less than twenty minutes later, everybody had cleared out, and Mike was ready to take the guy in.

"I appreciate you stopping me from..." Garrett gestured helplessly. "Thanks for getting here when you did."

"Thank your uncle," Mike said. "And next time you and Jessica have a fight, stay away from alcohol. Do you need a ride home?"

Hands on hips, Garrett hung his head and let out a self-deprecating laugh. "Believe it or not, I only had three beers."

Mike blew out a breath and shook his head. "Just make sure you head straight home or Sara'll kick both our asses."

He nodded. "I'll be in to give my statement in the morning."

Mike gave him a hard look, then steered his prisoner out the door.

Mandy appeared at his side again, this time with her purse and her keys. "Would you mind walking me out?"

"Course not." With a hand at the small of her back, Garrett escorted her out to the parking lot.

His truck was parked under an overhead light, and as

they got closer, he realized it sat at a funny angle. Almost as if...he rushed forward. "Son of a bitch!" He kicked the rim of his slashed tire and let out a string of curses that should've turned the air blue. One of the tires he'd just had replaced, too, dammit.

Mandy ran up beside him and grasped his arm. "Probably a friend of that guy. Come on, I'll give you a ride home."

Ten minutes later, they pulled up in front of his house. Completely exhausted, Garrett sat for a minute to collect his thoughts. First thing in the morning he'd have his truck towed to the Dodge dealer, and then he'd have to ask Sara for a ride to the station to give his statement. But first he needed sleep—and lots of it.

Before he realized her intentions, Mandy climbed over the console, straddled his lap, and wrapped her arms around his neck. "Ahhh, now this is better."

She wriggled her hips, dragging a groan from him. Hell, he wasn't made of stone...although if she didn't quit moving around he'd be able to do a pretty good imitation. He closed his eyes only to have Jessica's beautiful face visualize in his mind. *Damn her.* With a sigh of resignation, Garrett reached back to untwine Mandy's wrists from around his neck.

That's when she leaned forward and laid one on him.

Jessica waited until Wade fell asleep before slipping out the front door. She sat in the lawn chair and propped her bare feet up on the porch rails with a heavy sigh. Her life had done a complete one-eighty in less than twenty-four hours. My God, she'd barely survived the *last* time her life had plummeted out of control.

Marky.

Burying her son had been the hardest thing she'd ever done. Those first few months, she'd truly believed she would die of a broken heart. She hadn't eaten a bite of food the first week following his death and ended up in the hospital with an IV in her arm and her mother crying at her bedside.

Swiping away a tear, she shot to her feet and leaned against the railing. She still missed Marky every second of every day. He would have turned five years old this year. She probably would have bought him a bicycle for his birthday, and the biggest chocolate cake she could find. A rueful smile twisted her lips. She wasn't much of a baker, so the cake definitely would have been store bought.

She heard a vehicle approaching and saw the flash of headlights on her truck before an unfamiliar car pulled up in front of the Jamisons' house. Jessica squatted down and watched with interest. The overhead streetlamp cast just enough light to illuminate the people in the car—Garrett and an unknown woman. Jessica's heart dropped with a splash into her churning stomach.

Crouching down even lower, she held the wooden railing in a death grip, unable to look away. The woman, who sat in the driver's seat, climbed onto Garrett's lap and wrapped her arms around his neck. Then the slut leaned forward and kissed him.

Tears burning her eyes, Jessica clenched the railing so hard she caught a splinter in the thumb. *Dammit!* She stuck it in her mouth and tried to work it loose with her teeth as she watched the two of them go at it. A tear slipped down her cheek, and she angrily swiped it away.

No! She'd be damned if she'd shed even one more tear over the faithless jerk. He certainly hadn't wasted a second pining over her.

She inched back toward the front door and slipped into the dark house. Leaning against the door, she squeezed her eyes shut. Garrett had just given her all the proof she needed to see her original fears had been completely on the money. As of this moment, Garrett Jamison was officially out of her life. And as soon as she could make the arrangements, Wade would be as well.

Ten

Bang, bang, *bang*! Bang, bang, *bang*!

Jessica let out a long-suffering groan and rolled out of bed, landing on her knees. Who the hell could be pounding at her door so early in the morning? She worked her eyes open and glanced at the alarm clock; five-to-six. Damn, she hadn't even had four hours of sleep.

She climbed to her feet and grabbed her robe from its hook as she staggered out of her bedroom. Wade was muttering curses from the guest bedroom, and she flipped him off with both hands as she stormed by. Of course he couldn't see her through the shut door, but it felt good all the same.

She caught her reflection in the hall mirror and barely managed to stifle a scream. Her hair stood on end, her eyes were red and swollen from crying herself to sleep, and she had an indentation on her cheek that looked suspiciously like a pair of tweezers. *Tweezers?* Oh, yeah, she'd dug out that splinter while crying herself into exhaustion.

The banging started again. With a scowl, she stalked to the front door and swung it open—and had to cling to the knob for dear life as her knees threatened to buckle.

Standing on her porch, raking her from head to toe with those beady little eyes, was her ex-brother-in-law, Lyle Hastings. Her skin crawled and she felt as if the air had been sucked from her lungs.

"W-What the hell are you doing here?" she stammered, her voice an octave higher than usual.

Lyle shoved past her into the living room. "What do you think I'm doing here? Wade called. He asked me to come take care of him while you're at work. Didn't he tell you?"

"No, he didn't." Jessica's heart raced, and she struggled to get a hold of her emotions. Lyle scared the hell out of her—had since the night he'd cornered her in his mother's house after Wade had run out for some fast food. Thank God the older woman had arrived home before he'd had a chance to do anything more than feel her up.

Lyle turned to face her and smiled that loathsome smile of his. "Hell, if I didn't know any better, I'd think you weren't happy to see me."

"If you're here to take your brother home, then I'm ecstatic."

She walked past him into the kitchen without waiting for a response. She heard him go in search of his brother, and then the two of them whispering as she put on a pot of coffee. Her pulse sped up as she distinctly heard Wade say, *"Don't worry, she'll come around."* Having Wade here was hard enough. But Lyle staying under her roof, even for a short time, was more than she could handle. She'd die, though, before letting him see how rattled his presence made her.

She'd just poured herself a cup of her favorite dark roast when Lyle helped Wade into the kitchen and settled him on the chair to her right. Her former brother-in-law strode over to the counter, and after a short search, pulled two cups from the cabinet and filled both with her precious brew. She knew it was petty, but she resented them having even the one cup each.

"Morning, baby," Wade said, rubbing his eyes with his good hand. "What's for breakfast?"

Eyeballing him with disgust, she pushed the box of donuts across the table.

The brothers exchanged smirks. Lyle set both cups on the table and sat down across from her. Cripes, the man really did make her skin crawl. She took a sip of her coffee, then, unable to sit there a minute longer, got up to feed Mr. Louie—who'd yet to make an appearance. She sprinkled some dry cat food into his bowl and filled his water dish, but still no sight of him. Probably hiding in her closet.

If only she could do the same.

Jessica poured the rest of her coffee into the sink, then informed them, "I need to get ready for work."

Wade grabbed her arm as she walked past him. "You don't mind if Lyle stays for a few days, do you?"

"Would it matter if I did?" she countered, meeting his gaze. "Why don't you just let him take you home, Wade?"

"Because you and I have unfinished business."

"Bring something home for supper," Wade shouted as Jessica walked out the front door.

"Bitchy as ever," Lyle announced as her truck backed out of the driveway. "Lucky for her she's got big tits or no man would put up with that shit."

Wade grabbed one of his crutches with his right hand and pulled himself to his feet. "Forget about Jessie. We need to find that damn bear. I tried looking around yesterday while she was at work, but the pain meds hit me like a ton of bricks; made me groggy and dizzy as hell."

Lyle walked into the kitchen and opened the fridge. "No beer? You knew I was coming and didn't pick up any beer?"

"I have a broken arm and leg, you idiot. I can barely take a piss, but I'm supposed to run out and buy you beer? Besides, it's fucking morning. A little early to start drinking, don't you think?"

"Don't start riding my ass. You sound just like ma." Lyle started rummaging through the cabinets. "Jackpot," he said a minute later, pulling a bottle from the cabinet above the fridge. He held it up for Wade to see. "Wine. And I don't think it's cheap shit either."

"Like you'd know the difference," Wade muttered under his breath. Louder he said, "Well, pop it open and let's go. The sooner we find that bear, the sooner we can get the hell out of here."

"I figured you'd want to stick around for a while." Lyle searched through a couple of drawers until he found a corkscrew. "You haven't gotten laid in over two years. Unless, of course, you were nailing that cellmate of yours."

Lyle chuckled, and Wade threw a cat toy at him.

"Open that freakin' bottle already so we can look for the damn bear."

MEANT TO BE

"Here you go." Jessica set a hot beef and mashed potato plate on the table in front of her last customer of the day. Her shift ended in ten minutes and her feet couldn't be happier about that. "Can I get you anything else?" She met his gaze and was once again taken aback by the blatant interest in his eyes. He'd been mildly flirting with her since he'd come in.

"I wouldn't mind your phone number."

He had thick, curly dark brown hair and the most incredible eyes; sort of an olive green with flecks of amber around the pupils. He smiled, and Jessica realized she'd been staring. Her cheeks heated up.

"Sorry." She slid his check onto the table face down. "I didn't mean to be rude."

His smile widened, showing perfectly straight white teeth. "Hard to believe, but you're even prettier when you blush."

Jessica had to resist the urge to fan herself. She cleared her throat. Between Garrett, Wade, and Lyle, she had more than enough man trouble to keep her busy—and miserable. "Thanks. Listen, my shift is almost over, so if there's nothing else I can get you...?"

"How about that phone number? I'd love to take you out sometime."

In another lifetime, she would have given him her number in a nanosecond. But that was before Garrett Jamison had stolen her heart and ruined her for other men.

"I'm sorry, but I'm...seeing someone." Not a complete lie. She'd be seeing Wade as soon as she got home. Unless she got lucky and he and Lyle decided to head back to Seattle after all.

"Lucky man."

"Thanks." She managed a smile. "You have a good night."

Jessica headed to the back room to punch out, grabbed her purse, and chatted with one of the waitresses for a few minutes before heading out. The sun was still bright in the cloudless sky, and she had to shield her eyes as she crossed the parking lot to her truck. It wasn't until she reached it that she realized it sat at an odd angle.

"You've got to be friggin' kidding me!" Both tires on the driver's side were flat.

She stormed back into the restaurant and slammed her purse on the counter.

"What's wrong, sugar?" Angie Petrosky ran the register and answered the phone. She had salt-and-pepper hair up to the ceiling, a warm, motherly smile, and boobs so big it was a miracle she could stand upright.

"I have not one, but *two* flat tires, if you can believe it." Jessica grabbed the phone book from beneath the counter and flipped it open. "And they're both on the driver's side, so I'll need one of those flatbed tow trucks."

A shadow fell over the phone book, and she glanced up. Her green-eyed flirt stood in front of the register with his wallet out. He looked over and met her gaze before treating her to another of those great smiles.

"Everything all right?" he asked as he handed Angie a twenty.

"Just peachy." Jessica flashed him a quick, humorless smile. "I have two flat tires." She returned to the phone book and flipped to the T section.

"Here you go," Angie said, handing him his change. "Come again."

"You can count on it." He moved closer to Jessica.

MEANT TO BE

"Two flat tires? What did you do, park on a bunch of broken glass or something?"

She shrugged. "I didn't look." Sheesh, she had no idea who to call. She'd never needed a tow truck before.

"I could make the call for you," he offered, as if sensing her confusion.

Jessica smiled her relief. "Would you? I'd be so grateful."

Thirty minutes later, she watched her truck get hauled away by a twenty-four hour towing company. Time to call herself a cab...or she could spend the night at a hotel and let the Hastings brothers fend for themselves. Ah, hell, with her luck they'd probably hunt her down.

"Can I give you a ride home?"

Jessica smiled up at her green-eyed savior. He stood about six-feet-tall and had a muscular build. Not bulky like Garrett, but whipcord lean.

"I appreciate the offer, but I've imposed on you enough."

"I'm not a serial killer, if that's what's worrying you." He grinned and held up his hand, palm forward. "Scout's honor."

The man's smile was contagious. And truth was the thought never crossed her mind. God couldn't be that cruel, to make a man this gorgeous a criminal. "I just feel like I'm taking advantage. You've already wasted almost an hour of your time, and you must have better things to do than chauffeur me around."

"I have a hot date with my recliner to watch a ballgame," he teased. "But I'm sure it won't mind if I see you home first."

Jessica laughed. "I don't know what to say, you've been great."

"My intentions aren't completely selfless," he admitted with a lopsided grin. "I figure a ride home gives me a little more time to talk myself into a date."

She shook her head and held out her hand. "Maybe it's time we introduced ourselves. Jessica McGovern."

He took her hand in both of his then brought it to his lips. Jessica playfully rolled her eyes.

"Jack Sutton, at your service."

"What the hell is *he* doing here?" Garrett grumbled as he poured himself a cup of coffee. He grabbed a couple of the chocolate chip cookies Sara had dropped off earlier and took a seat at the kitchen table. Mr. Louie sat on the counter looking entirely too comfortable. Damn, the last person he wanted to think about tonight was Jessica, yet here sat her cat, staring at him as if in condemnation.

Nicky shrugged. "Not sure. He's been here all day. It's almost like he's afraid to go home."

Garrett's gaze turned curious. "What's the matter, boy?" he said under his breath. "You don't like her newest bed partner?"

"Newest bed partner?" Nicky echoed. "What the hell are you talking about?"

"Nothing. Mind your own business."

His brother pushed up from the table and carried his coffee mug to the counter. "You gonna tell me what happened last night? Uncle Luke thinks you and Jessica had a fight, and I'm assuming he's right."

"You know what they say when you assume something."

Nicky topped off his coffee. "Yeah, except you're the only ass in this room."

All of a sudden, Mr. Louie jumped off the counter and ran to the back door. He meowed and scratched at it almost in a frenzy.

Garrett and Nicky exchanged glances.

"Guess he's ready to go home," Nicky commented.

Curious, Garrett got up and opened the back door, but the cat just stood there staring up at him. "What? If you want to go, go. I'm not gonna hold the damn door open all night."

Mr. Louie stepped outside, then turned back and looked up at Garrett as if he wanted him to follow him.

"Crazy cat," he muttered before setting his cup on the counter and following the mammoth fur ball outside.

Mr. Louie led him around to the front of the house, and Garrett realized with a tightening of his chest that Jessica stood out by the curb, talking to yet another man. Damn, he'd give anything to be able to turn back time and snap on a condom. How the hell could he have been so wrong about her?

He was halfway down the driveway when he saw two men standing on her front porch. *Jesus, she's got a fuckin' harem.* One he'd never seen before, but the other he recognized as the jerk-off from last night.

Mr. Louie stopped and looked back, as if to make sure he was still following. Garrett cocked a brow. If he didn't know any better, he'd swear the cat made a 'let's go' motion with its head.

Jessica looked up as he approached, and Garrett was taken aback by the hostility in her eyes. What the hell? He'd practically caught her in the act with the gimp standing on her porch, yet she had the nerve to look at him as if *he'd* betrayed *her*?

She's nuts, man. Just be thankful you found out now.

"Your cat seems to have forgotten where he lives," Garrett said when he reached her, flicking a dismissive glance at her newest conquest, then at the guy's car. The old Buick looked vaguely familiar. He returned his gaze to the owner, surprised to find the idiot staring at him with nearly as much hostility as Jessica. She must have told him some whopper of a tale.

Jessica bent down and gestured for Mr. Louie who leapt into her arms. She stood, stroking the cat's head, looking pretty damn uncomfortable as her gaze moved from Garrett to the men on her porch.

The gimp remained leaning against the railing while his friend hopped down and strode toward them. He cast a quick glance at Garrett before turning his full attention to Jessica, his expression hard. Jessica watched him approach, and Garrett could have sworn she clutched Mr. Louie even tighter, as if in support. No vehicles were parked in her driveway, so he couldn't even run the plates to find out who this idiot was.

But he *could* run the plates of her newest conquest's car.

"What's going on, Jessie? You're an hour late. We were starting to worry."

She shot a look at Garrett before explaining. "Someone slashed a couple of my tires. I had to have my truck towed, and Jack here was kind enough to offer me a ride home."

Garrett's hackles went up. Jessica ends up with two slashed tires the day after he does? *Coincidence? Doubtful.* Just what the hell was going on? Had he stepped into an episode of *The Twilight Zone*? Within twenty-four hours, his life had done a complete turnaround, and nothing made a damn bit of sense. At least he had one set of plates and a first name to work with. Garrett watched as Jack transferred his hostility to the numbnuts standing in front of Jessica. This whole scenario was getting stranger by the second.

The guy from her porch reached out and cupped Jessica's elbow. Mr. Louie hissed and swatted at him. Garrett and Jack both took a step toward her, but Jessica held up a hand to ward them off. She turned to Jack. "Thanks for everything. Hopefully, one day I can repay the favor."

Garrett snorted. He knew exactly how she'd be repaying the guy.

She then turned the full force of her displeasure on him. "I'm sorry Mr. Louie's been bothering you. I'll do my best to make sure it doesn't happen again." With one last look at Jack, she rushed up to the house.

Numbnuts gave Jack and Garrett each a 'stay the hell away' look before following Jessica inside, leaving the two men alone on the curb.

"She's scared of those two," Jack commented, still watching the house.

"Trust me, she'll be fine."

The guy turned a look of contempt on him before returning his attention to the house. Garrett stared at his profile, convinced he knew him from somewhere, but damned if he could recall where. "Do I know you?" he finally asked.

Jack didn't respond for almost a full minute. Finally, he met Garrett's gaze and said, "Check your guilty conscience. I'm sure you'll figure it out."

Before he could find his tongue, Jack hopped in his

car and took off.

Memorizing the guy's plates as he drove away, Garrett thought, *Yep, I've definitely entered The Twilight Zone.*

Garrett had just hung up from ordering Chinese food when the phone rang.

"The tags belong to a Jack Sutton," Mike said without preamble. "Released from Green Bay Correctional about a week ago after serving seven years for murder. And if that doesn't jog your memory, you were a key witness to the case."

He leaned back against the kitchen counter and pinched the bridge of his nose. "I remember now. I found him unconscious next to one of my old partner's informants, Eddie Morales. Morales had been shot between the eyes, and Sutton was holding the murder weapon."

He also recollected he'd thought the crime scene had looked like a set-up, but he'd been a rookie at the time, and frankly, scared to death of his ex-partner, Marty Driscoll. Garrett had seen and heard enough suspicious activity to know Officer Driscoll was a less than honorable cop. But he'd been well-respected by his peers, and the one time Garrett had voiced his opinion, Driscoll had quickly put him in his place. Two years later, he'd transferred down to Atlanta, and Garrett couldn't have been happier.

"Think he's out for revenge?" Mike asked.

"That'd be my guess. Both mine and Jessica's tires were slashed within twenty-four hours of each other. And

Jack just happens to be there to offer her a ride home? No, he's definitely got an agenda." He refilled his coffee cup. "There's just one thing that bothers me. He seemed...genuinely concerned for her safety. I think she may have told him something about those two morons who've taken over her house."

"But she had to have just met him," Mike pointed out. "Why would she confide in a complete stranger over you?"

Garrett carried his coffee to the table, sat down, and propped his feet on the chair across from him. "Let's just say it's complicated." He blew out a weary breath. "Listen, thanks for your help. Last night as well."

"No problem. Give me a call if you need anything else."

Garrett clicked the OFF button and set the cordless on the table. As he sipped his coffee, he flipped back through his mind's rolodex to Jack Sutton's trial. The guy had been maybe eighteen, nineteen years old when he'd gone on trial for murder. Garrett recalled how scared he'd looked sitting at that table next to his incompetent public defender, without even a single family member in the courtroom to support him. He'd sworn he was innocent, insisted he'd been set up. And though there'd been no way to prove it, Garrett had suspected the kid was right. Unfortunately, he couldn't testify on his gut instinct, only the cold hard facts.

Now that kid was a grown man with a hate-on for Garrett the size of Texas. And he couldn't really blame him. It had been his testimony of the facts presented that had sealed Jack's fate.

It finally struck Garrett why Sutton's car looked so familiar. It was the same one that nearly mowed him down in front of the restaurant. The guy'd had seven years of vengeance driving him, only at the last second he'd swerved away. The only question that remained was…why had he decided to go after Jessica?

Garrett's gut instinct told him Sutton wouldn't hurt her, though he'd learned the hard way his gut instinct was less than reliable. But the guy had seemed truly worried about her. So, why the slashed tires? And what had been the point of slashing Garrett's tires other than to piss him off?

Only one way to find out. He needed to discover where Jack was staying and pay him a little visit.

With grim determination, he redialed Mike's number.

Jessica's truck was delivered within the hour. She'd had to pay extra, but there was no help for it. She only had one vehicle, and it would've cost just as much to take a cab back and forth to work the next day, plus tip.

Lyle had ordered a pizza as soon as they'd entered the house. She waited until after the food arrived before locking herself in her bedroom and jumping in the shower. She knew Lyle was less likely to launch an assault on her if he had an extra-large pepperoni pizza to keep him occupied. Plus, he and Wade were both a little buzzed after having drunk her special occasion bottle of wine. Cripes, was nothing sacred?

As she stood under the steaming hot spray, she racked her brain, thinking up ways to get those two out of her house—ASAP. She couldn't even imagine what the neighbors must think of her. She'd traveled halfway across the country to escape the public hell her life had become. People pointing and staring, the pity in their eyes more than she could take. And now here she was, on the verge of becoming the talk of the neighborhood all over again.

Jessica dressed in baby blue sweats and a T-shirt, pulled her hair up into a ponytail and didn't bother with any make-up.

Not surprisingly, they'd devoured the entire pizza, leaving her not even a single sliver of crust. Biting the inside of her cheek, she strode past them into the kitchen, dug a can of tomato soup out of the pantry and made herself a grilled cheese sandwich to go with it. Only the grilled cheese reminded her of Garrett, and she was struck by an overwhelming urge to cry. She'd give anything to be able to turn back the clock and not pick Wade up from the hospital.

Then the memory of that woman sitting on Garrett's lap while they sucked face caused her tear ducts to pucker shut as a spark of anger fanned slowly to life. The unfaithful jerk had waited all of a couple hours before finding comfort in the arms of another.

Shaking off all negative thoughts, she decided to get a load of laundry going. She headed downstairs, but switched directions when she realized one of her work uniforms was out in the truck.

Someone shouted her name just as she reached the curb. She looked up and saw Garrett's sister jogging toward her, Ethan right on her heels. Jessica stopped and blew out a hard breath. She liked Sara. Very much, in fact. But she just wasn't in the mood to have this particular conversation. Sara adored Garrett and no doubt intended to rip Jessica a new one for daring to hurt her precious brother.

"Hey, I was hoping we could talk for a minute," the redhead said when she'd reached her.

"Listen, I know what you're going to say, but—"

Sara held up her hand and shook her head. She glanced down at Ethan and said, "Sweetie, why don't you go on in. I'll be there in a few minutes."

The kid wrinkled his little brow, but did as he was told.

"I just wanted to make sure you're all right. I know you and Garrett had a falling out, but that's all I know. Garrett won't tell any of us what happened."

Jessica didn't know what to say. She'd been sure Sara meant to chastise her for the whole Wade incident. "I'm fine, really. And I appreciate your concern." She glanced over in time to watch Garrett open the door for Ethan. The eldest Jamison cast them a curious look before disappearing back inside the house. She felt the familiar sting of tears and quickly returned her attention to his sister—lest she embarrass herself by falling to pieces right there on the sidewalk for all to see.

"But you're not going to tell me what happened either," Sara guessed with a rueful smile.

"I'm sorry. I just don't see the point. Garrett made his choice, and so did I." Jessica smiled in an attempt to lighten the mood. "I hope you and I can remain friends, though. I mean, if you'd still like to."

The woman threw her arms around her and gave a surprisingly hard squeeze. Jessica hugged her back with just as much fervor. She really liked her new friend and was grateful she wasn't holding a grudge. Then, remembering what Garrett had confided to her at the restaurant, Jessica pulled back and looked down at Sara's stomach. "I'm sorry, I didn't mean to hurt you." *Crap, that's right, I wasn't supposed to know.* Oh, well, it wasn't as if Garrett could get any more mad at her than he already was.

Her distress must have shown on her face because Sara grinned and assured her, "It's fine. I kind of figured he'd tell you."

"I'm so happy for you. Mike and Ethan, too. They must be pretty excited."

Sara made a face. "Mike was thrilled once he got past his initial shock. Ethan? Not so much. He's not exactly happy about having to share his father."

"Don't worry, he'll get over it."

"I know."

An awkward silence settled over them. Jessica thought about the little keepsake she kept in the glove box of her truck. Marky's first toy, which she'd bought when she was six months pregnant. She'd stuffed it in there the day she'd hit the road for Green Bay, and hadn't been able to bring herself to look at it since.

"Hang on a sec." Jessica stepped over to her truck and opened the passenger-side door. She pursed her lips in contemplation as she eyed the glove box. It was a big step. Sort of like giving away her emotional crutch. And while she wasn't exactly sure why, she wanted Sara to have it. She had a feeling it would be a step in the right direction for herself as well.

Jessica opened the glove box and pulled out the precious brown teddy bear. Turning to Sara, she held it out and said, "I'd like you to have this. It belonged to my son."

A frown creased Sara's brow. She accepted the bear and lovingly stroked its little ears. "I don't know what to say. I had no idea you even had a child."

Jessica grabbed her uniform out of the truck and shut the door. None of them knew, not even Garrett. But somehow, she knew it was time. "Marky died more than two years ago. This was the first toy I ever bought him." Tears stung her eyes. "He slept with it every night. Couldn't sleep unless it was clutched in his little fist."

"Jessica, I can't accept this. I'm honored, truly, but it obviously means too much for you to let it go."

"No, I want you to have it. I know you don't understand...neither do I, really. I just know I want you to have it. Please."

Her friend gazed down at the little brown bear for a moment, then looked up, a tremulous smile curving her lips. "Thank you so much."

After a quick, watery hug, Sara disappeared into the Jamison house and Jessica into her own. She stopped and leaned against the door for a brief moment, to gather herself. Then strode inside to face the devils.

Eleven

As soon as Sutton opened the door, Garrett threw an uppercut that would have felled an ox. The guy flew backward onto the bed, rolled off, and landed against the far wall with a thud.

"What the fuck was that for?" Jack demanded as he climbed to his knees. "Shit, I think you broke my jaw—"

"You tried to run me over, you slashed my tires. Jessica's, too. Take your pick. You should be grateful I'm such a forgiving guy." Garrett slammed the door shut behind him.

Jack snorted. He stood up and tested to make sure his jaw still worked. "You stole seven years of my life. I should've run your ass over and never looked back." He walked over to the sink and checked his face in the mirror.

Garrett glanced around with disgust. A twinge of guilt that he was at least partly responsible for Sutton's present situation gnawed at him. Not purposely responsible, of course, but if he hadn't been so afraid for his family, he would have followed his instincts.

"You were found unconscious next to a corpse with the murder weapon in your hand."

"Yeah, your buddy, Driscoll, did a great job of setting

me up. And you had the easiest job of all. Accidentally stumble onto the crime scene."

What could he say? Driscoll *had* sent Garrett to check out the abandoned warehouse he'd found Jack and Eddie Morales in. Garrett distinctly remembered a chill had run up his spine. He'd only been a rookie at the time, but he'd still thought the crime scene looked suspiciously like a set-up. And it hadn't helped that Garrett already suspected Driscoll of being involved in shady dealings.

"You weren't the only one who was set up," Garrett finally muttered.

Jack strode over and gaped at him. "What the hell are you saying? Are you admitting—"

"I'm not saying anything. Look, you were convicted of murder by a jury of your peers. You were found unconscious with the murder weapon in your hand."

"Yeah," Jack said, "I must have fainted right after I plugged Morales."

Smartass. "I admit, it seemed a little strange. But I'm a cop, and I deal with facts. And the facts were I found you lying next to the victim with the murder weapon in your hand."

"Tell me, did they check for gun residue on my hands?"

"I'm sure your lawyer explained to you those tests are inadmissible in court."

"Exactly as I figured. No test was done, and my good-for-nothing lawyer was no doubt paid off by Driscoll, that rat bastard."

Garrett blew out a hard breath. "Look, I don't know whether you were set up or not. But either way, I had nothing to do with it."

Jack stared at him, obviously struggling to believe

Garrett's claim. "Your testimony put me behind bars."

"I told the truth, plain and simple."

Jack let loose with a derogatory laugh as he dropped down into the dark-green, padded armchair. "You said exactly what Driscoll wanted you to say, whether you knew it or not. Everybody did what Driscoll said or they ended up like Morales."

Garrett propped his hands on his hips. Sutton was right and he knew it. And the bitch of it was, there wasn't a damn thing they could do about it. Driscoll was long gone, and certainly way too smart to have left behind any evidence linking himself to the murder.

"Driscoll transferred to Atlanta years ago, so I doubt you have anything to worry about. Maybe you should just be thankful you didn't end up like Morales and get on with your life. You're a young guy—"

"Don't you fucking patronize me." Jack shot to his feet and swiped his fingers through his hair. "I'm supposed to be *thankful* that prick stole seven years of my life? I'm supposed to just let him get away with it?"

"Look, I understand your frustration, but what else can you do? Driscoll is connected in ways you don't want to know about. You go after him, and you'll come back to Green Bay in a body bag."

Jack's eyes narrowed. "You sure do seem to know a lot for someone who claims he's not in Driscoll's pocket."

"I heard and saw enough to know I'd be foolish to cross the guy."

"So, you turned your back while he set me up. Nice. Real fucking nice."

A muscle ticked in Garrett's jaw. Sure, he'd suspected a setup the moment he'd walked into that warehouse. But he'd been a rookie, and Driscoll a well-respected officer with over fifteen years on the force. Who would have believed him, let alone agreed to investigate the matter? Garrett had had his suspicions and nothing more.

And Driscoll had guaranteed Garrett's silence with one blood-curdling comment. *"That's one fine looking sister you got there, Jamison. Sure be a shame if anything happened to her."* The threat had been crystal-clear. And Garrett would've died before putting any of his family in jeopardy.

"If it makes you feel better to blame me, fine. I really don't give a shit. But I'm only going to say this once. If you come within fifty feet of Jessica again, I'll break every bone in your goddamn body."

Wade and Lyle both passed out by nine o'clock. They'd killed a twelve-pack of beer between them, on top of the wine, and Jessica couldn't have been happier. She'd tried to get to sleep herself, but after tossing and turning for more than an hour, all she'd managed to do was tear the sheets from her bed. After shrugging into her robe, she grabbed a bottle of water from the fridge and slipped out the back door.

Mr. Louie had refused to step one paw inside the house with the Hastings brothers still there, and she found him curled up on top of the patio table. Jessica gave him a quick scratch behind the ears before plopping down on one of the padded lawn chairs.

She heard a vehicle pull into the Jamison's driveway and scowled. As tempted as she was to hide, a surge of pride kept her planted firmly in the chair. It'd be a cold day in hell before she hid from the likes of Garrett Jamison. Besides, he'd have to walk around back to have a chance of even seeing her, and that was unlikely.

Before she could stop him, Mr. Louie jumped off the table and took off down the driveway, meowing his little lungs out the entire way.

"Traitor," she muttered under her breath. She'd just decided to slip back inside when Garrett appeared from around the corner of the house, Mr. Louie in his arms.

"Your cat seems to think I'm his new best friend." He glanced around before adding, "So, where's *your* new friend? Or should I say *friends*?"

The faint glow of the porch light illuminated his handsome face, and Jessica hated the leap in her pulse. "Not that it's any of your business, but he's my *ex*-husband. And the other guy is his brother."

Garrett looked surprised by that bit of news. He'd truly believed she was some kind of slut who collected strange men like trophies? *Jackass*.

He cleared his throat and set Mr. Louie down on the grass. Annoyed to no longer be the center of Garrett's attention, Mr. Louie gave his paw an angry lick, then took off like a shot.

"So, you and your ex are reconciling," Garrett said, his tone casual, his expression dispassionate. "And you wanted to get one last fling in before he got here. Not that I'm complaining, but you could've mentioned it before jumping into bed with me."

"I thought I'd made my position perfectly clear," she reminded him, stung by his callous attitude. "Friends with benefits, nothing more."

He stared at her, hard, as if trying to glean the truth through mental telepathy. Finally, he gave a curt nod and said, "Yeah, you were clear. Nothing more. Have a nice life, Jess." Garrett turned and strode away.

"We're not reconciling," she blurted before she could stop herself. "I hate that man more than you can imagine." Damn, why couldn't she have just let him go? As disappointed in him as she was, Garrett didn't deserve to be led on.

She placed her hand over her belly as the thought that she could be carrying his child reared its head—and it wasn't exactly unwelcome. Jessica realized with a start that she wanted another child. Garrett's child.

He stopped, but didn't turn around. "Are you purposely trying to drive me nuts? I mean, has that been your plan from the beginning?"

She took a deep breath and let it out slowly. "I tried to tell you last night, but you were in such a rage—"

He finally swung around to face her. "What did you expect me to do? Join in?"

"Don't be disgusting," she snapped. "Nothing happened. Nothing was going to happen. He'd been in a bus accident. Didn't you wonder why he was in an arm and full leg cast?"

Garrett dropped his arms to his side and flexed his fingers. "Trust me, it was...more than obvious he thought something was going to happen, broken limbs or not."

Her face heated up. She uncapped her water and took a sip, then held the cold bottle against her throat. "Wade says he came here to win me back, but like I said, it'll never happen. And since I'm the only person he knows in the entire Midwest, the nurse called me. I agreed to let him stay for a few days until he could travel back to Seattle. His brother's here to take care of him while I'm at work, and then escort him home. *That* is all there is to it."

"Why didn't you just tell me this yesterday? Or earlier today?"

She cocked a brow in disbelief, and Garrett surprised her with a soft chuckle. He took another step toward her. "So...what exactly are you saying, Jess?"

"I'm saying you're a hotheaded jackass." An image of that woman straddling his lap flashed in her mind. "And a faithless jerk, too."

He closed the distance between them and stood before her with his arms crossed. "I jumped to the same conclusion anyone would have under the circumstances. You can't exactly blame me."

"Yes, I can."

An arrogant grin curved his lips. Jessica shot to her feet and sloshed water onto the front of the oversized T-shirt she wore as a nightgown. "Dammit." She set the bottle on the table and plucked the fabric away from her skin. "Look what you made me do."

"Do I make you that nervous?"

"You make me that crazy."

He reached out and pulled her into his arms. "Well, that makes it mutual, now doesn't it?"

Jessica opened her mouth to protest just as he leaned down and captured her lips. He wasted no time in plundering her mouth, the hot, raspy feel of his tongue on hers enough to weaken her knees. Her nipples tightened and tingled against his hard chest, and she silently wished he'd strip off her wet T-shirt and replace it with his mouth. A groan escaped her at the thought.

Garrett held her flush against him with a hand at the small of her back, then reached between them and cupped her breast over the damp material. His tongue played with hers as his fingers teased her nipple, plucking it gently before moving on to torture the other. When his other hand curled around her bottom and squeezed, she gasped and grew wet.

Jessica tried to slip her hands between them to unbutton his jeans, but Garrett stopped her. Instead, he guided them around his neck before returning his attention to her body. Deepening the kiss, he reached beneath the hems of both her robe and nightshirt and grasped her waist. He kneaded his way down to her hip, gave it a squeeze, then worked his knee between her legs and spread them apart. Jessica shivered in anticipation.

He skimmed his hand around to the front of her panties and stroked her throbbing flesh. She wiggled against him, silently begging him to explore further. Garrett used the tips of his fingers to caress her through the material, back and forth, up and down, until she thought she'd faint from the pleasure of it. Their kisses grew more urgent, and she ran her hands up into his thick hair, cupping his scalp. He slipped his fingers beneath the elastic of her panties and pulled them aside, exposing her hot, bare flesh. Finally, he sank his fingers between her wet folds.

Her knees gave out, and she had to hold on for dear life as he stroked her clitoris with his palm while working his fingers deeper into her slick passage. He slid one finger in, then pulled it back out ever so slowly, repeating the process until he'd built up a rhythm, and she found herself moving in time with his finger.

Jessica tried to break free so she could unzip his pants and inflict a little torture of her own, but Garrett seemed in no mood to relinquish power. He swept her backwards until she found herself lying on her back in the cool grass, staring up at the stars. The faint, sweet smell of petunias clung in the air, and the chirping of crickets played like a symphony in the background.

"Garrett?"

"Shhhh. Just close your eyes and relax." He pulled her robe down so that it was between her and the grass, and then lifted up her nightshirt. "Now I owe you two pairs," he whispered a split second before tearing her panties off with one mighty rip. He grasped her knees to spread her legs wide. Jessica closed her eyes and licked her lips in anticipation. He worked his hands beneath her bottom, then lifted her up an inch or so off the ground.

The first stroke of his tongue was nearly her undoing. Jessica bit her bottom lip to keep from crying out as he licked back and forth between her folds while kneading her backside, intensifying her pleasure. His tongue flicked over her clitoris, and Jessica's hands clenched in the cool, dry grass as she moved her hips against his mouth. He ate her with hungry abandon, licking, stroking, sucking, until Jessica thought she might faint from the sheer—

Her back arched like a tightly strung bow as he brought her right to the brink of ecstasy. "Yes...oh, my...*Garrett*..." Whimpering, her head whipped from side to side as she tore up clumps of grass with her fists.

He lifted her even higher, and she cried out when his mouth closed over her clitoris and sucked hard. Clutching his hair with both hands, she came so hard she thought her heart stopped.

Garrett continued to stroke her throbbing flesh until she lay still, her breathing ragged, her heart pumping furiously.

Eyes gleaming in the dark, he gently closed her legs

and pulled her nightshirt down, as if to somehow preserve her modesty. She almost laughed at the thought. He then dropped down beside her and gathered her in his arms. They lay together staring up at the stars.

Jessica curled into his side. "Would 'thank you' sound lame?"

He chuckled. "No, and you're welcome." He tightened an arm around her and kissed the top of her head. Mr. Louie decided to join them and parked himself on Garrett's chest. He scratched behind her cat's ears and joked, "At least he has good timing."

Jessica slipped back into the house a short time later and hurried down the hall to her bedroom. The house was as dark and quiet as when she'd left it, and she breathed a sigh of relief as she closed her bedroom door behind her. She flipped on the bedside lamp and gasped. Wade stood propped up against the wall opposite the bed—and the look in his eyes was glacier.

"Jesus, you scared me half to death," she breathed, holding a hand to her pounding chest. "What the hell are you doing in my room?"

"I warned you, Jessie. I told you to stay the hell away from him."

Jessica's blood froze in her veins. "Y-You were watching us? You disgusting—"

"What kind of whore have you turned into? Letting him go down on you like that, on the ground, for crissake."

Anger replaced her dismay. "You have the nerve to pass judgment on me? Our son would still be alive if you hadn't been screwing the neighbor!"

Wade's eyes narrowed. He pushed off the wall and hobbled toward her on one crutch. "You want to bring that shit up again? Fine. And where were you when Marky fell off the counter?"

Tears stung Jessica's eyes. "Shut up. Just shut your mouth. How dare you bring that up. I was trying to earn a living. Keep a roof over my son's head and food in his belly. Something you were too lazy to do."

Wade stopped a couple feet in front of her. "You stay the hell away from him or I swear I'll—"

"You'll what?" she snapped. "File harassment charges against him? It'll be your word against his, and he's a cop. And if you think I'll back you up, think again."

Wade's expression became even more hostile. He surprised her by changing the subject. "Where's that stuffed bear Marky used to sleep with every night?"

"What?"

"The brown bear with the dark blue ribbon around its neck. Where is it?"

She frowned and crossed her arms over her chest. "Why do you care?"

"Dammit, Jessie, where is it?"

She dropped her arms and sighed. "I'm in no mood for this, Wade. Just go back to bed."

He surprised her by giving her a shove with his crutch. "I said, where's the goddamn bear? I'm not playing. I want it right now."

Jessica darted out of his way and stared at him in shock. As big a jerk as he was, Wade had never laid a hand on her in violence. Why was he so anxious to get his hands on Marky's bear? "I gave it to a friend. Why? You've never shown an interest in our son's things before."

"Never mind. Just get it back from whoever you gave

it to."

With that, Wade hobbled from the room, giving the door an angry crack with his crutch on the way out. Jessica wanted to follow after him and demand to know exactly why he wanted that particular toy, but was too relieved to have him gone. Not only did she hate having to look at him, she was mortified that he'd actually been watching while she and Garrett...*my God.* The thought made her skin crawl.

"I'm embarrassed to even ask this, but...can I have that little stuffed bear back?"

With a knowing smile, Sara opened the door and motioned Jessica inside. "No need to be embarrassed. It was too soon to part with it. I completely understand." Her friend waved her into the kitchen and motioned for her to have a seat at the table.

Having just gotten off work, Jessica wanted nothing more than to eat her supper and relax in front of the TV. And at first, she'd had no intention of getting the bear back for that disgusting ex of hers. But she'd hoped that once he had it, he'd head back to Seattle, and she'd never have to look at his face again. "I feel so silly, but...you're right. I wasn't ready."

Sara poured them both a glass of lemonade, then said, "Be right back."

She returned a few minutes later, her brow creased in puzzlement. "I can't find it. I swear I set it on my dresser, but it's gone. I wonder if Ethan decided to play with it." She walked to the French doors and stuck her head out. "Ethan, get in here, please."

MEANT TO BE

Ethan scampered inside, his smile faltering when he caught sight of Jessica. "What?"

"Do you know where that bear is? The one Jessica gave me for the baby?"

He cast Jessica an odd look before shrugging his shoulders. "I dunno."

Sara crossed her arms over her chest and cocked a brow. "Where's the bear, Ethan?"

Jessica almost smiled. Ethan obviously couldn't put a thing past his mother, and the red stain creeping up his neck was all the proof needed that he knew exactly where the bear was.

"I-I was playing with it, and it accidentally fell in the mud."

His eyes grew bright, and though she seriously doubted the bear landing in the mud was an accident, Jessica felt bad for him.

Sara cast her an apologetic look. "Ethan James, go get the bear. I'll throw it in the washing machine." She looked back at Jessica. "I'm really sorry."

"Don't even worry about it. I'll wash it." She smiled at Ethan. "Could've happened to anyone."

"But I don't have it." Ethan shuffled his feet and glanced longingly at the back door, no doubt wishing he were anywhere else in the world. "I gave it to Muriel. She said she'd make it look good as new."

Sara frowned. "Uncle Luke took Muriel out for dinner and a movie. They probably won't be back for hours."

Jessica waved it off. "No problem. I'll get it from her tomorrow."

"Dammit, Jessie, I want that bear back tonight!"

She walked past Wade into the kitchen and put on a pot of water for tea. Lyle stared at her from the table, his face expressionless, his gaze so intense she could nearly feel his filthy hands on her. She resisted the urge to race into her bedroom and lock the door.

"Wade, I know that bear has no sentimental value for you, so why don't you just tell me the real reason you want it."

He glanced at Lyle who gave an almost imperceptible shake of his head. Wade hobbled toward her on his crutch. "None of your damn business. Just go get that bear, and I mean now."

She avoided looking at him as she dug a new box of tea bags out of the pantry. "The bear is in one of the neighbor's houses. It's a long story, but I'll get it for you tomorrow. Then you and your brother can get the hell out of my house and out of my life." She finally met his gaze. "For good."

A sneer curled Wade's upper lip. "I'd be nice to me if I were you. I have a feeling your cop boyfriend wouldn't so much as spit on you if he knew what you used to do for a living."

"You rotten bastard," Jessica whispered, her throat constricting with long buried shame.

"Not that I'm into strippers." Garrett's words replayed in her mind, and she knew he could never know about her short-lived past profession.

"Who has the bear, Jessie? Tell me, and we'll be out of here by tomorrow. Don't, and I let all your new friends know just what kind of a slut you are." Wade hobbled over to the table and slowly lowered himself onto a chair. He picked up his cell phone, and motioned her forward. Jessica could only watch in stunned silence as Wade clicked picture after picture. The man had a slide show of her and Garrett in the backyard!

Jessica stared at him, tears burning her eyes. How could she have ever thought she loved this man? She knew exactly what the two of them would do if she told them who had the bear—break into Muriel's house. The only question was, why were they so desperate to get their hands on it? Did it really matter, though? Muriel and Luke were out on a date, so it's not as if anyone would get hurt. And then, she would be free of the two of them for good.

"Fine, you win. But after I tell you, I want those pictures deleted."

TWELVE

Jack watched with interest as one of Jessica's houseguests appeared from around the side of her house and crept across the darkened lawn, being careful to stay out of the glow of the streetlights. Instead of climbing into her, which was parked in the street, he continued down the block until he reached the second house from the corner. After a quick look around, he snuck up the driveway and disappeared from sight.

Jack opened his car door and did a fast jog toward the house, arriving just in time to see the guy climb in through a side window. Having just served a seven-year sentence, Jack was more than reluctant to follow him inside. But he didn't have a cell phone, and the idiot would probably be long gone before Green Bay's finest morons showed up.

A strangled scream followed by a loud thump took the decision out of his hands. Jack hoisted himself through the window and crept up the stairs. He came upon the guy standing over an unconscious woman lying on the floor. He looked up at Jack, and his deer-caught-in-the-headlights expression would have been comical if his hand hadn't been resting on the zipper of his pants. *The sonofabitch.*

Jack tackled him without second thought.

Garrett wasn't sure why Sutton was sitting in his car watching Jessica's house, and while he didn't exactly trust the guy, he didn't believe he was a threat either. But when he shot out of his car and ran down the street and up Muriel's driveway, Garrett knew he couldn't take any chances. He put in a quick call to the station, grabbed his pistol, and raced down the block after him.

He approached cautiously, not wanting to do anything foolish. The window on the side of the house that led into Muriel's guest bedroom stood open, and just as Garrett leaned in to take a look, a body crawled out as if the hounds of hell were on his heels. Garrett grabbed him by the back of the neck and yanked him out the window. Sutton. *Damn.*

"Let me go, you moron, he's getting away!" Sutton delivered a quick jab to Garrett's mid-section and tried to jerk free.

Garrett grunted but held onto Sutton with all his might.

"Nice try, asshole. You know, I was willing to give you the benefit of the doubt until I realized you were casing Muriel's house—"

"It wasn't me," the ex-con insisted as he struggled to free himself. "Didn't you hear what I said? He's getting away thanks to your incompetence." Jack let out a string of curses, before finally settling down.

As soon as Garrett relaxed his grip, Sutton threw a punch that nearly knocked him off his feet, then took off running just as two squad cars peeled into the driveway, blocking his escape. All four officers jumped from their respective vehicles and advanced on him, guns drawn.

"Down on the ground, now!" Officer Hank Hamilton demanded. Without taking his eyes off Sutton, he said, "Hey, Jamison, what the hell's going on?"

Garrett stuck his own pistol back into the waistband of his jeans and made his way to Sutton's side. He shook his head, more disappointed than he cared to admit. "Possible B&E. I caught him slipping out the side window. Couldn't have been inside more than a few minutes, though. And Muriel's out with Uncle Luke, which Sutton here already knows since he's been sitting in his car across the street for the past few hours."

"You're making a huge mistake," Jack insisted from his facedown position on the driveway. "I didn't break into this house. I was following one of the idiots staying with Jessica. Go check inside and see for yourself. There's a woman lying unconscious in the upstairs hallway."

Garrett's heart skipped a beat. Muriel? Couldn't be, she was out with Uncle Luke. He raced around to the back, yanked open the screen door, and kicked in the door. "Muriel?" he called out as he sped up the stairs. His breath rushed out in relief when he saw her, leaning up against the wall, her head cradled in her hands. He dropped to his knees beside her.

"Jesus, are you all right?" He gently checked the back of her head. She winced when he found the goose egg-sized knot behind her left temple.

"I-I think so. I'd feel a whole lot better if my house would quit spinning."

Garrett helped her to her feet and into the bathroom. "You were attacked. Do you remember what happened?

And where the heck's Uncle Luke?"

Muriel laid her forehead against the side of the bathtub and let out a low groan. "We headed up to Krupp's for a drink before supper when my daughter called and asked if I could babysit Haylee. Luke dropped me off and then ran across town to pick up Culver's. Haylee loves their french fries."

Jack had been sitting in his car for at least three hours, so he had to have known Muriel was home. Why would a guy who'd just been released from prison after seven long years risk a trip back to the slammer for something as stupid as burglary? Especially a young guy with his whole life ahead of him?

"Any idea who assaulted you?" Garrett stepped past her and glanced out the window. Hamilton and Dreyer had Sutton cuffed and sitting in the back of their squad car, and the second squad was just backing out of the driveway. He turned back to face her.

Muriel climbed slowly to her feet and wet a washcloth. She held it against her goose egg with a grimace. "No clue. I saw a shadow move beside me, and I screamed. That's when I got clunked on the head." She frowned. "So, how did you know to come check on me? Did you catch the perp?"

"I caught a guy climbing out your window, but he swears he's not the one who attacked you. That's why I was hoping you'd seen him." That, and Garrett had a strong feeling Sutton was telling the truth. "Hamilton and Dreyer have him in custody out front. I'm sure they're just waiting on word about you before hauling him in to the station."

"I'm sorry, I wish I could help."

"I'm just glad you're all right. I think we'll have you

checked out at the ER, though, just to be safe."

Muriel shook her head and then groaned, grasping onto the bathroom sink for support. "I can't. I'm watching my granddaughter tonight, remember?"

"Sara can watch Haylee until you get back. Ethan would love the company. And Uncle Luke should be back soon, so I'll have him run you up to St. Mary's." When she looked as if she would argue, he added, "Don't even waste your breath."

Jessica panicked when she heard the back door slam shut, then Wade and Lyle whispering furiously. A sense of dread drove her from her room in search of answers. She stepped into the living room in time to see Wade whip a beer can at Lyle's head.

"You fuckin' moron! Couldn't keep it in your pants, could you?"

"What in the world are you talking about?" Jessica demanded, looking from one to the other.

Lyle scowled at her, then walked into the kitchen and grabbed a beer from the fridge. "I'll go back for it another night," he said, ignoring her question.

"Christ, you're dumb as a box of rocks." Wade shook his head, then hobbled over to the window and peeked out.

That's when Jessica realized red and blue lights were dancing across the walls.

She strode past him to the front door. "What are the cops doing—"

"Get away from the door," Wade snapped, shooting another look of disgust Lyle's way.

"Dammit, Wade, I wanna know what's going on right now. He was supposed to grab Marky's bear and..." Wade's words of a moment ago finally sank in. *Dear Lord, please, it can't be. She wasn't supposed to be home!* "Tell me he didn't hurt Muriel. Wade, tell me she's all right!"

"Oh, stop with the dramatic bullshit," Lyle said as he collapsed onto the rocker-recliner. "She's fine. I clunked her on the head, but before I could look for the bear, that idiot who drove you home the other day showed up and jumped me." He took a swig of his beer, and an evil smile twisted his lips. "He's being arrested right now by your next-door neighbor. How funny is that?"

Bile rose in her throat. Lyle's black, soulless eyes were enough to give her nightmares for life. She took a deep shaky breath and escaped into the kitchen. If the scumbag was telling the truth, Muriel was safe, but Jack was being arrested for saving her from Lord only knew what. The injustice of it made Jessica want to scream.

Once Muriel was on her way to the hospital, and a thrilled-to-be-able-to-stay-up-late Ethan was teaching Haylee how to play Combat Commando, Garrett climbed in his truck and headed to the station.

Hamilton sat at a desk punching in the police report while Sutton slumped forward in his chair, hands cuffed behind his back, quietly resigned. When he walked up, Sutton flicked him a disgusted look, but remained silent.

Garrett sat down next to him, leaned back, and crossed his arms over his chest. In a low voice he said, "Let's just say, for argument's sake, I believe you. That still doesn't tell me why you were staking out Jessica's house. Didn't I tell you to stay the hell away from her?"

Sutton remained stubbornly silent. Garrett gave him a full minute, then stood up and said, "Don't say I didn't give you a chance."

He took two steps before Sutton finally spoke. "She's scared. Those two aren't staying in her house because she invited them."

Garrett sat back down and propped his elbows on his knees. "Care to elaborate?"

The ex-con shrugged. "She made a couple of odd comments the other day when I drove her home from the restaurant. When I asked her where she lived, she said, 'Hell, at the moment.'"

"Not exactly a surprising comment considering it's her ex-husband. If living with him were heaven, they'd probably still be married."

With a quick shake of his head, Sutton said, "You didn't see her face. She wasn't just annoyed or put out. She was scared, plain and simple."

Garrett frowned and leaned back in his chair. Could the guy be right? Could Jessica be in some sort of danger with those two staying in her house? The thought drove a bolt of fear straight up his spine. "You're sure it was her ex's brother who attacked Muriel?"

"Positive."

"So the guy's a thief. Great."

"Maybe."

Garrett frowned. "Something else you'd like to share?"

"Depends." Sutton met his gaze. "You gonna let me sit in a jail cell for something I didn't do? Again?"

"Don't even go there." Garrett let out a disgusted

sigh. "Fine. Spill."

Sutton cast a quick glance back at Hamilton, then leaned forward in a conspiratorial manner. "Bastard was about to rape her. He was standing over her unbuttoning his fly when I got there."

Garrett's heart stopped. Jesus H. Christ, he was going kill the sonofabitch with his bare hands! He shot to his feet and raced from the police station, ignoring Sutton's angry shout. He'd give Hank a call later and have Sutton released. Right now, he needed to make sure Jessica was safe.

Wade and Lyle flipped on the television to watch for any late-breaking news. Jessica was too worried to try and sleep, so she grabbed a bottle of iced tea from the fridge, her laptop from the bedroom, and sat down at the kitchen table.

She opened the laptop and had to stifle a scream. Garrett's reflection stared back at her in the screen, and she quickly realized he was standing outside her kitchen window behind her. She spun around, and he motioned her over. Pulse racing, Jessica leaned back and chanced a quick glance into the living room. The Hastings brothers were both engrossed in the news. She tiptoed to the back door, slowly turned the knob, and inched it open.

Mr. Louie shoved his way in with a howl and ran straight for his food bowl. Jessica closed her eyes and waited for her racing heart to slow. Then she started inching the door open again.

"Where the hell do you think you're going?"

Jessica swallowed a shocked gasp and turned to face

Lyle. "Mr. Louie was scratching at the door, so I let him in. What? Am I a prisoner in my own home now?"

Ignoring her, Lyle tossed his empty beer can in the trash and grabbed another. Wade hobbled into the kitchen as someone rapped on the door.

"Answer it," Wade ordered. He limped up behind her and gripped her shoulder. "And don't forget, you're just as guilty as Lyle."

Bastard. He was right, though. She'd wanted these two out of her house—and her life—so badly, she'd put her own needs ahead of Muriel's safety. Taking a deep breath, she swung the door open. Garrett stood on the porch, his eyes narrowed on Lyle. He looked ready to commit murder.

"You got a problem?" Lyle said as he cracked open his beer.

Garrett cast her a quick glance, his gaze taking in Wade's hand on her shoulder, then returned his attention to Lyle. "You're my problem. You broke into one of the neighbors' homes and attacked her. You're going to pay, too, you sonofabitch."

"You're crazy. I was here all night."

"She saw you. Described you to a T."

"You're full of shit—"

"He hasn't left the house all night," Wade said, cutting Lyle off. "Ain't that right, baby?" He gave Jessica's shoulder a warning squeeze.

She stared at Garrett, apologizing with her eyes as she nodded agreement. His expression was inscrutable. If Muriel had seen and identified Lyle, then Garrett knew Jessica was lying. She could only hope he'd be able to forgive her when all was said and done.

"You're coming with me," Garrett said to her. "Let's

go."

Wade gave her another warning squeeze.

It took every bit of strength she had to keep her wits about her. As much as she wanted to walk out with Garrett and never look back, she knew that wasn't an option, for many reasons—the most important being she had no idea what Lyle might do if pushed. She needed to get Marky's bear back ASAP so they would leave her in peace to live her life—secrets intact.

"Please," she insisted. "Just go. I'll be fine."

"There's no way in hell I'm leaving you—"

"I mean it, Garrett. I want you to leave."

"You heard the lady," Wade said, dropping his hand and stepping back.

Garrett shifted that inscrutable gaze between the three of them before landing on Lyle. "Harm one hair on her head, and you're a dead man." With that, he turned and strode away.

Lyle stepped forward and slammed the door shut. "Self-important asshole."

Jessica spun around and glared at both of them. "You've been in town less than a week, and you're already in trouble with the cops, not to mention you've turned me into a liar. Dammit, I want you both out of my life!" She grabbed her laptop and stormed from the kitchen.

Garrett arrived at Mike and Sara's front door just as Uncle Luke and Muriel were leaving with Haylee, who was fast asleep in the older man's arms. A bittersweet smile touched Garrett's lips. Uncle Luke had given up so much to raise them, and for the millionth time Garrett was humbled by his sacrifice. Especially since he knew Uncle Luke would have made a wonderful father if he hadn't had his brother's four kids to raise.

He shifted his gaze to Muriel. "I take it you're all right? No concussion or anything?"

"Right as rain. I've got a rock-hard noggin."

"Thank God." Garrett looked back at his uncle. "Take care of these two."

"You bet. In fact, I'll be staying the night, just to be safe, so don't expect me home."

Garrett gave him a quick thump on the shoulder.

He found Sara sitting at the kitchen table with a baby book and a glass of milk looking oddly radiant considering the late hour. "Ethan sleeping?" he asked as he sat down across from her.

She smiled at him and closed the book. "Yeah. He and Haylee passed out about an hour ago. Want some coffee?"

He leaned back in the chair and laced his fingers behind his head. "Thanks, but I'll pass. I'm going to have enough trouble trying to sleep tonight."

Sara's smile faded. "Poor Muriel. I can't believe something like this happened right on our own block. So, who's this Jack guy anyway?" When he raised a questioning brow, she said, "I called Hank about an hour ago."

Garrett frowned. Hank had always been putty in Sara's hands. "Jack Sutton. It's a long story, but bottom line is he swears he's innocent. Says he saw Jessica's ex-brother-in-law break into Muriel's house, and he followed him inside." No point telling her the full story. Lyle wouldn't be stupid enough to try anything again tonight, and Garrett would be sure to explain the situation to Mike first thing in the morning. "So, where's the man of the house?"

"Fell asleep just before the kids." She grinned. "They wore him out making him give them piggyback rides up and down the stairs."

Garrett chuckled at the mental image. He'd wait and call first thing in the morning to talk to Mike.

Sara suddenly looked thoughtful. "You don't think...no, forget it, can't be that."

"What? Come on, spill."

"I don't know. Just seems odd that he would break into Muriel's house the same day Jessica came asking for the bear back."

"'Asking for the bear back?' You lost me."

"Jessica gave me a little plush bear that belonged to her son. I sensed she wasn't ready to part with it—it's only been a couple years since he died—but she insisted. And sure enough, she came by earlier asking for it back. That's when I found out Ethan had decided to play with it and"—she made the quote signs—"accidentally dropped it in the mud. He gave it to Muriel to wash, no doubt hoping I wouldn't find out."

Garrett stared at her, waiting for the punch line—praying for the punch line. *Her son?* Jessica had a deceased son that she'd never bothered to mention to him? Yet she'd told Sara, and his sister obviously assumed Garrett knew or she wouldn't have said anything. And what the hell was so important about this bear?

Only one way to find out.

"Listen, I need to speak with Uncle Luke quick before he heads to bed. Tell Mike to give me a call tomorrow before he leaves the house."

There was a rap on the door just as Muriel snuggled up in Luke's arms on the sofa. She huffed her annoyance and started to get up.

"I'll get it," Luke said as he rose to his feet. "Can't be too careful."

Muriel smiled at him, amazed by her good fortune. Luke Jamison was a king among men, and he was hers.

She just needed to convince *him* of that.

He returned to the living room with Garrett in tow.

"Hey, beautiful. I'm sorry to bother you, but I need that bear Ethan gave you to wash."

"Oh, that's right. Sara said Jessica had asked for it back. Poor thing." She got up and went into the laundry room. She'd washed the bear inside the linen bag she used to wash her unmentionables, and it looked pretty darn good, even if she said so herself.

Garrett was in the process of giving Luke a thump on the back when she returned. *Men*, she thought with a shake of her head.

"Here you go." She handed him the bear. "And please don't be mad at Ethan. It truly was an accident."

Garrett lifted a brow. "I'm not mad at him, but we both know it wasn't an accident."

Muriel grinned. "Well, maybe not. But he's had a lot to deal with this past month, and he isn't ready to share his daddy just yet. Try to understand."

"I do, don't worry."

Garrett chucked her under the chin, and she did a mental eye roll.

As soon as Luke closed and locked the front door, Muriel sidled up next to him and wrapped an arm around his waist. "Since I can't mix booze with the pain meds they gave me, I think I'll pour myself a glass of ginger-ale. Care to join me?"

Luke met her gaze without reservation, sending a tingle of awareness straight to her toes. "Don't mind if I do."

When they were once again settled in front of the TV, Luke pulled her up against his side and held her close. Muriel closed her eyes, giddy with excitement. Her shy guy was loosening up a little more each day. At this rate, it wouldn't be long before—

"Do you have any idea how scared I was when I saw that cop car in your driveway with its cherries flashing?" he said, his voice thick.

Muriel looked up and met his gaze. His eyes smoldered with emotion; his intent clear. She reached up and cupped his cheek at the exact moment he leaned down to kiss her. His mouth slanted across hers, his tongue tracing her lips, seeking entrance. Muriel moaned and opened for him. She'd wanted this man for so long, had yearned for him from the moment they'd met. And here he was, kissing her breathless, holding her so tight she thought she might burst into flames.

She positioned herself so she was astride his thighs, then twined her arms around his neck and gave in to the sweet sensations coursing through her. Her blood felt like molten lava as it flowed through her veins; every nerve ending on high alert.

"I'm not hurting you, am I?" he whispered against her cheek.

"Not even a little bit," she said, thankful for the

prescription of pain relievers she'd gotten from the hospital.

Luke moved one hand from her waist down to cup her shorts-clad bottom. *Please*, she thought, *let tonight be the night*. He squeezed, and she gasped. How could she have ever thought this sexy man was gay?

He broke off the kiss and whispered in her ear, "I want you. Is the feeling mutual?"

Muriel nearly groaned her relief. "You know it is."

"Thank God."

Muriel hung on for dear life as Luke shot to his feet and carried her to her bedroom. He pushed the door open with his elbow and carried her inside, then leaned back to shut it.

He sat on the edge of the bed, and Muriel untangled herself from his lap. She knelt in the middle and met his gaze as she slowly unbuttoned her blouse. Luke swallowed, that gorgeous brown gaze following her every move. She slid her blouse off her shoulders and tossed it aside, then reached back to unclasp her bra. He kicked off his boots, then lied back against the mountain of pillows and watched her through heavy-lidded eyes.

"You're so beautiful," he whispered. "Come here."

Muriel had nice breasts, and she knew it. But the blaze of approval in Luke's eyes was more than she'd hoped for. She crawled toward him, her breasts swaying, and smiled her satisfaction when a low, drawn-out growl escaped him. He leaned forward and grasped her upper arms to drag her across his lap. Muriel laughed softly as he flipped her onto her back. He smoothed one callused hand up her stomach, between her breasts, gently cradling each one before looking up to meet her gaze.

"I have protection."

She bit her bottom lip suggestively. "I hope you have more than one."

He chuckled and pulled his wallet out of his back pocket. After a quick inventory, he teased, "Think three'll be enough?"

"Maybe," she teased right back. "But I'll be making up for lost time, so it'll be close."

"You and me both," he admitted, his voice thick.

With that sexy grin she couldn't get enough of, Luke tossed his wallet on the nightstand and returned his attention to her breasts. He circled her sensitive flesh with his index finger, trailing a scorching path around and around until he reached her tingling nipple. With reverent care, he leaned down and captured it with his lips, his tongue stroking over the areola.

Eyes closed in ecstasy, Muriel tangled both hands in his hair, arching into him, moaning her pleasure. He reached up with his other hand and started working her shorts down her hips. She lifted in an effort to aid him, wanting to be naked beneath him more than she'd wanted anything in a very long time. He tossed them aside, then went right back for her panties. Within seconds, she found herself completely naked...and oddly vulnerable.

"Your turn," she said, trying to work his shirt off his back.

Luke mmmmed as he released her nipple. He sat up and peeled off his T-shirt, then stood and reached for his zipper. And the tease took great pleasure in slowly unzipping his jeans, working them down his impressively muscled thighs.

Her pulse picked up speed. The proof of his desire for her strained against the front of his boxer-briefs, begging to be free.

Muriel sat up in a rush and said, "Let me. It's like my birthday and Christmas all rolled into one."

Luke laughed softly and shook his head. "Woman, you are great for a man's ego."

She met his gaze and caught her bottom lip between her teeth. Then grasped the waistband of his briefs with both hands and unwrapped her present.

Garrett sat down at the kitchen table and examined the plush bear. It wasn't very big, maybe ten inches tall, brown with a dark blue satin ribbon around its neck. Its belly felt especially hard, as if overstuffed, which wouldn't have been odd if the head, arms and legs had all been similarly tight.

Holding the bear by its tummy, he gave it a squeeze. *Yep, definitely something inside.* He gave it a shake to see if it squeaked or something. Nope. Flipping it over, he examined each seam. Between the legs, the thread was a different color. The stitch job was surprisingly good, but Garrett had no doubt it had been opened and stitched back up.

He retrieved a thin-bladed knife from the block on the counter and carefully slit the bear's crotch open. Once the hole was large enough, he slipped his forefinger inside and felt around, less than surprised when his finger tapped something solid. He carefully sliced a few more threads, taking special care since he knew the item once belonged to Jessica's deceased child—even if he was still a little stung that she hadn't trusted him enough to share something so important.

His hand stilled, the slap in the restaurant suddenly

making sense. Garrett's face burned with shame as he recalled his insensitive comment. *No wonder she never told you about her son, you idiot.*

No time to dwell on it now. He worked the small package out with great care, but it was impossible to tell what it was since it had been wrapped in duct tape. Garrett stuck the tip of the knife in and slit it open, careful not to slice too deep. Beneath the duct tape was a layer of plastic wrap, and when he finally peeled it all away, a tiny, black felt bag sat on the table. He loosened the drawstring and shook the contents out onto the table.

Garrett let out a slow whistle. Three diamond rings twinkled up at him, and although he was no expert, he knew they had to be worth a fortune. *Jesus*, he thought as he picked one up and examined it more closely, *you could buy a yacht with the money one of these suckers would bring in.* Each ring had a huge center diamond surrounded by a dozen or so smaller stones. And they must be real diamonds. Why else would they have been so carefully hidden?

He realized something else was stuck in the bag and was less surprised to pull out a very small square of folded up cash which had been taped. He carefully peeled the tape away and unfolded the one-inch bundle to discover six one-hundred dollar bills.

Setting the money down next to the rings, he pinched the bridge of his nose. Garrett knew Jessica couldn't have known what was inside the bear or she wouldn't have given it away in the first place. And earlier, the way her ex had hovered behind her, he'd been purposely intimidating her. But how? What could he possibly be holding over her head to make her lie for him? Because she *had* been lying. Lyle had attacked Muriel, not Jack.

And the sonofabitch was going to pay. Garrett would see to it.

But first he needed to get Jessica the hell out of that house.

Thirteen

"It's not my fault that idiot brother of yours got caught," Jessica said as she slipped into her soft-soled work shoes. "I have bills to pay, and if I call in sick, Mr. Turner will fire me without a second thought. I'm already on his bad side."

"I don't give a damn, Jessie. I don't trust you, and I don't trust that overgrown, corn-fed guard dog of yours. He knows damn well Lyle attacked your neighbor, but he ain't got a stitch of proof. And I can't afford to have him 'lick' some sense into you."

She shot Wade a glare over her shoulder. "You're a disgusting pig."

"And you're a slut. Believe me, I want out of this hellhole as badly as you want me gone. But I ain't leaving 'til I have that bear."

Jessica snatched her purse off the counter and swept past him. Lyle had set out on foot for McDonald's—thank God he couldn't drive a stick shift—and Wade would have to tackle her to stop her from leaving. Since she didn't see that happening, she felt confident in her escape. She needed out of this loony bin her home had become. If Lyle made one more sexually lurid gesture, she swore she'd start screaming and never stop.

She knew as each day passed, temptation grew, and the chance of Lyle assaulting her became closer to a reality. And Lord knew Wade would be of no use to her. Even if a kernel of decency remained in him, he was in no condition to take on anyone.

"Well, thanks to Lyle, your chances of getting it back today are slim to none. You'll have to wait until Muriel returns it to Sara, and Sara returns it to me. *If* they haven't already figured out that's what Lyle was after." She fished her keys out of her purse. "I'll be back after my shift...unfortunately."

Wade didn't utter a word as she strode out the front door.

For the first time since the slapping incident, Jessica was looking forward to heading in to work. Her shift was the busiest of the day, which would keep her mind occupied and unable to dwell on whatever chaos might be going on in her house.

"Hi, Uncle Garrett!"

Garrett glanced up from his coffee and smiled. "Hey, sport. You're out and about early."

Ethan pulled the screen door open, skipped to the table, and plopped onto his favorite chair. "Yeah. Well, Mom's puking so Dad said I could come down here for breakfast." He leaned across the table and helped himself to a chocolate glazed donut. "Oh, and Dad said he'll call you as soon as Mom quits puking."

The little stinker grinned, and Garrett shook his head.

"How about a glass of milk to go with 'breakfast'?" He got up to pour it without waiting for a response. He set the glass on the table just as his nephew leaned forward to snatch Jessica's bear off the Lazy Susan.

"Muriel's awesome, it looks brand new!" he said, flipping it around to examine it from every angle.

"That she did. Listen, sport, I need to jump in the shower. Why don't you run downstairs and get in some practice with Combat Commando. Won't take me no more than ten minutes. And if your dad calls, just ask him to come down when your mom is feeling better."

Wade stuffed the last of his Egg McMuffin in his mouth and tossed the wrapper in the bag. "Ain't no way around it. If we send Jessica over for the bear, they'll put two and two together."

Lyle sipped his coffee, his expression mutinous. "I swear to God, before we blow this burg, I'm breaking that Jack dude's neck."

"Hey, you got no one to blame but yourself. Always thinking with your dick. If you'd just waited until the bitch was gone, we'd have the bear and be on our way home."

"Christ, you gonna harp on that shit all night?"

Wade glared at his brother and shook his head in disgust. "Dumb as a box of rocks."

"Me? I ain't the one who went to prison for killing my own kid."

"You know goddamn well it was an accident," Wade growled, wishing he had the use of all four limbs so he could kick Lyle's worthless ass.

His brother leaned back and kicked his feet up onto the coffee table. "Yeah, I forgot. You were banging the next-door neighbor, and he fell off the counter. Great dad you turned out to be."

"You heartless—"

There was a knock at the back door. Lyle pulled his feet off the table and slowly sat up. "Who the hell could that be?"

"Only one way to find out," Wade said. "Don't worry, they can't arrest you without any proof, and you said she never saw you." He grabbed his crutch and climbed to his feet, coming up behind Lyle just as he opened the door.

They both stared down in stunned silence at the little boy who wore much the same expression they no doubt wore—and the kid had Marky's bear clutched in his fist.

Since he knew God wasn't likely to grant him any favors, Wade figured this had to be some sort of trap. But would they really use the kid like that? Highly doubtful. The boy must have run over on his own to return the bear.

"Hey, little man, whatcha got there?" Wade asked as Lyle stepped aside.

"Jessica's bear. Uncle Garrett had it on his table. He was prolly gonna give it back, but since I'm the one who dropped it in the mud, I figgered I should say sorry."

"That's awfully grown up of you. I bet your Uncle Garrett's real proud." Wade motioned for Lyle to let the kid in. "Jessica just ran to the store for cookies and ice cream. I bet she'll be real happy to see you when she gets back. What's your favorite kind of cookie?"

The kid stepped into the kitchen, peered curiously up at Lyle, then skipped over and took a seat at the kitchen table. "Chocolate chip. Uncle Garrett's, too. I bet Jessica's buying chocolate chip cookies."

With a jerk of his head, Wade gestured for his brother to shut and lock the door. "Bet you're right. Jessica's nice like that. Right, Lyle?"

"Yep. Real nice," his brother absently agreed. He pulled back the ugly sunflower-patterned curtain and took a quick glance outside before heading into the living room.

Wade lowered himself onto the chair across from the kid, but never took his eyes off Lyle. He watched with mixed emotions as his brother withdrew a handgun from his duffle bag and stuck it in the waistband of his jeans. He stood up, made sure his shirt covered the gun, and strode back into the kitchen.

Wade heaved an inner sigh. The last thing he wanted was for the kid to get hurt, so without further ado... "Hey, mind if I check out that bear?"

Ethan leaned forward and tossed the bear across the table. Wade scooped it up and gave it a squeeze. His smile faded. *That sonofabitch.* Lyle caught his eye, his gaze questioning. Wade shook his head. Lyle punched the air and signaled for Wade to join him as he stalked into the living room.

"Hey, buddy, I have to run to the little boys' room. Why don't you help yourself to some milk. That way you'll be ready for dunking as soon as Jessica gets back with the cookies. Clean glasses are in the dish drainer."

"Okay."

Wade grabbed his crutch and climbed to his feet. He nearly tripped when Jessica's big, ugly cat ran into the kitchen and jumped onto the table.

"Mr. Louie!" The kid slid off his chair and hugged the mangy thing. Even more strange, the cat let him. *Well, at least it's good for something*, Wade thought as he hobbled into the living room.

"Call that bitch right now," Lyle said in a furious whisper. "We need to get those rings back before Paul Bunyan hands 'em over to the cops."

Wade leaned his head back and checked on the kid. Good, he was still preoccupied with the cat.

"Hand me the phone."

***

"W-What did you say?" Jessica stood behind the cashier's station, the phone glued to her ear, her heart in her throat. Dear God, she couldn't have heard him right.

"I said, get your ass home now or the kid watching TV with Lyle isn't gonna make it home for supper tonight," Wade repeated, sounding unnaturally nervous.

Jessica swallowed hard and wiped her clammy palm on her uniform. "Wade, he's an innocent kid. What the hell were you thinking?"

"I'm thinking I want my goddamn rings back. And they're not in the bear, which means your cop boyfriend has them. Get home, Jessie. *Now*."

"What rings?" Jessica heard a click, then a dial tone buzzed in her ear. She tried to hang up the phone, but her hand shook so bad it took her three tries before it hooked onto the cradle. Frozen in fear, it took her another moment to gather her wits. Then she raced to the back room and threw open the office door.

"Mr. Turner, I am truly sorry about this, but I have an emergency at home and I need to leave right away. My neighbor just called. A pipe burst and my basement is flooding." *Please have a heart and let me go.*

Mr. Turner squinted his displeasure and leaned back

MEANT TO BE

in the chair, fingers steepled atop his rounded belly. "Ms. McGovern, you know I can't let you leave when there's no one here to cover for you. If you leave, don't bother coming back."

Without hesitation, she unpinned her name tag and slapped it on his desk.

Jessica raced out of the restaurant and blew four stop signs on the way home. The thought of what that disgusting pervert could do to Ethan sent an ice-cold chill up her spine. *Calm down.* They wouldn't dare harm a hair on his head. Not if they wanted the rings Wade had mentioned back. And not unless they had a death wish, because Garrett would kill both of them with his bare hands if any harm came to his beloved nephew.

Garrett. If he could look her in the eye without wanting to vomit after this was over, it'd be a miracle.

She deserved his contempt. Thanks to her, his entire world had been screwed with, and now his nephew was in danger. And it was doubtful he was even aware of the latter or that call would've been from the morgue asking her to come identify Wade and Lyle's bodies.

All looked peaceful and calm as she turned onto her street. She parked in front of the house, managing to do so without squealing the tires in her haste. After casting a quick, assessing glance next door, she ran up her driveway, hoping that maybe, just maybe, she could end this without a single act of violence.

Wade stood with the back door open, an impatient scowl twisting his handsome features. "About goddamn time," he muttered, grasping her arm to hurry her inside.

"I lost my job thanks to you," she said as she tossed her purse on the counter. "Where's Ethan?"

Wade gestured toward the living room. She took a

deep breath and plastered a reassuring smile on her face before heading in.

Ethan and Lyle sat on the couch, with Mr. Louie's fat frame sprawled out between them. *Good kitty*, she thought, knowing exactly what that wonderful feline was doing—protecting the little boy. If Lyle so much as touched the kid, he'd have twenty-two pounds of hissing, scratching fur ball to contend with. The thought gave her only a moment's relief since she knew Lyle wouldn't hesitate to shoot her cat.

She cleared her throat. "Why, hello, Ethan. What brings you by?"

He looked up and smiled, the most genuine smile he'd ever directed her way, which only made her feel ten times worse.

"I brung over your bear. I'm sorry I dropped it in the mud, but look." He plucked it off the end table beside him and proudly held it up. "Good as new. Muriel's the best, huh?"

"That she is," Jessica agreed. "And thank you for bringing it by. But I think I'd better get you home. Do your parents know where you are?"

"They think I'm at Uncle Garrett's, but when he took a shower, I figgered I'd come bring you the bear. It was sitting on the kitchen table, so I bet he was gonna bring it to you."

"I bet you're right." *And to tell me to stay the hell out of his life.*

"The kid stays here," Lyle said, uncrossing his arms and draping one over the back of the couch above Ethan's head as if in silent warning. "I'd advise you go 'thank' Uncle Garrett, and thank him long and hard if that's what it takes, you got me?"

Ethan gave her a curious look, and she countered with a reassuring smile. He scratched Mr. Louie behind the ears, his expression thoughtful. "Can I have some cookies? Did you buy chocolate chip?"

Jessica looked back at Wade who deadpanned, "Ethan showed up right after you left for the store to buy cookies and ice cream. You must have left the bag in the car."

"Uh, yeah, I did. I'll go get it right now." She swept back into the kitchen and eyed Wade with all the contempt she could muster.

Thank God she had an unopened bag of Chips Deluxe in the pantry.

Garrett trotted down the stairs dressed in only a pair of jeans, and refilled his coffee cup. "Hey, sport," he called out. "Think you got in enough practice to take me on?" He'd gotten stuck on the phone twice before he'd even made it into the shower, so Ethan was no doubt ready for battle.

The phone rang yet again. Garrett rolled his eyes and grabbed the cordless off the wall as he headed toward the stairwell that led to the basement. "Hello?"

"Garrett?"

"Yeah? Who's this?" He glanced downstairs and frowned when he realized the lights were off. Had Ethan run back home?

"Listen, it's Jack. I just followed Jessica home from work, and it's a damn miracle she made it in one piece. Blew practically every stop sign on the way. Something's definitely going on and—"

"Whoa, slow down." Garrett walked through the

house, glancing in each room as he went. "What the hell are you talking about? Why did you follow her home from work?" A bad feeling mushroomed in his gut. What could cause Jessica to race home from work, no doubt risking her job in the process? His gaze happened to land on the Lazy Susan, and his heart missed a beat. Jessica's bear was missing.

"I followed her to work," Jack said. "Planned to keep an eye on her; make sure she's safe. About an hour later she comes running out of the restaurant and jumps in her truck. She drove home so fast I could barely keep up with her."

Jesus H. Christ, Ethan! Garrett's stomach lurched. "Can you see into the house from the road? Is there a young boy with her?"

"The drapes are closed, I can't see anything. Why?"

Garrett cursed and snuck a peek out the window. Her kitchen curtains were drawn as well. *Please, God, not again.* "I think those two scumbags snatched my nephew."

"Why the hell would they do that? They got a death wish?"

"No, they needed insurance. I have something they want back real bad."

Jessica set six cookies on a small plate, but when she opened the fridge, Wade informed her, "He already has milk in the other room." Then he mouthed the words, *Hurry up.*

She set the plate on the coffee table and said, "Ethan, I need to run over and speak to your Uncle Garrett for a minute, then we'll both be back, all right?"

Without looking up from the TV, Lyle replied, "Ethan and I will be waiting."

Wade grabbed her arm as she attempted to sweep past him. "I don't care what you have to do to get those rings back, just do it. I can't guarantee the kid's safety in my condition, and I don't need to tell you what a nutjob Lyle is."

He stared at her hard, and Jessica swallowed a sob.

"If anything happens to Ethan, you and Lyle are both as good as dead."

"That's why this is all resting on your head. Get the rings back, and no one'll get hurt. Lyle wants out of this place as much as I do, trust me."

"I can't believe you sullied your son's memory like this."

Jessica couldn't be sure, but she thought a twinge of regret crossed Wade's features.

"He was still alive when I...never mind. Just get your ass over there. The sooner you get back, the sooner we can all get on with our lives."

She took one last look at Ethan, grateful to see Mr. Louie now perched on his lap. Then, with a deep breath, she yanked open the back door—and came face-to-face with Garrett.

"Where is he?" he demanded, stepping past her into the house. Wade tried to hobble out of his reach, but it was no use. Garrett grabbed him by the front of his shirt and slammed him against the counter.

"Uncle Garrett, why—"

Jessica turned in time to see Lyle haul Ethan off the couch, sending Mr. Louie flying in the process. He reached behind his back, and before she could blink, he had a gun pressed to Ethan's head. Jessica cried out in protest as Garrett roared.

"You sonofabitch!"

"Take one step and he's dead."

"U-Uncle Garrett? I didn't mean—"

"It's okay, sport, this isn't your fault. Just relax. No one's going to get hurt." He looked at Wade. "Right?"

"Exactly right. Just hand over my rings and cash and we can all go about our business."

Garrett reached into his front pocket and pulled out a little black bag. "Stolen, I presume?" he said as he tossed the bag to Wade.

"Stolen? Nah, these belonged to our grandma. Ain't that right, Lyle?"

"Yep. On our mother's side."

Garrett's expression was carefully controlled, but Jessica knew what it cost him to remain calm. Her heart ached for him, and for his nephew who visibly trembled as tears streaked down his face. To Wade, she said, "You got what you came here for. Let Ethan go and please, just…go."

Wade quickly checked his loot, holding each ring up to examine in the sunlight spilling in though the mini blinds. Then he counted the cash and smiled. "All right, Lyle, you can let the kid go. Jessie, you'll be driving us to Seattle."

"What? You got what you wanted, what do you need me for?"

"I just said, to drive," Wade snapped. "You know Lyle can't drive a stick, and I have a buyer for the rings up in Minnesota."

"Over my dead body," Garrett stated and started forward.

Lyle brought the gun up and pointed it at Garrett's head. "Believe me, cop, that can be arranged."

"You leave my Uncle Garrett alone!" Ethan demanded, struggling to free himself. Lyle gave his arm a hard jerk, which brought fresh tears to Ethan's eyes.

Jessica took a deep breath and tried to reason with him. "Lyle, please, let him go. The sooner you let these two go, the sooner we can pack and be on our way. Hell, I'm tired of this town anyway."

It was Wade who said, "Fine. Go grab what you'll need and hurry the hell up."

"No goddamn way," Garrett stated, and Jessica was afraid of what he might do, especially since Lyle still had a hold of Ethan.

"You ain't got a choice, Paul Bunyan." Lyle gestured toward the door that led to the basement. "Now get your ass down there. Jessie'll call your sister once we're safely out of town and tell her where you and the kid are."

When Garrett made no move toward the basement door, Lyle aimed the gun back at Ethan's head. "Don't try my patience."

Wade hobbled forward and grasped the doorknob. He opened it, and someone sprang out and tackled him to the ground.

Jack!

Out of the corner of her eye, Jessica saw Ethan break free from Lyle and run toward Garrett—at the same moment Garrett pulled his own weapon.

She threw herself in front of the boy just as Lyle squeezed off a shot.

Fourteen

Garrett knew raw terror as Lyle took aim at his nephew and pulled the trigger. In that split second, Jessica dove in front of Ethan and took the hit herself. He fired as Lyle attempted to escape out the front door. A blood stain blossomed dead center on his back, and he collapsed face down on the floor. Garrett retrieved Lyle's gun, then made sure Jack had Wade under control before dropping to his knees to examine Jessica's injury.

"Sport, I want you to run home and tell your dad to get down here as fast as he can, all right? Tell him I already called 911."

Which he did as soon as he heard the back door slam in Ethan's wake.

"She okay?" Jack asked as he knelt down beside her.

"I'm fine," Jessica insisted, attempting to sit up.

She bit her lip and squeezed her eyes shut, and Garrett wished he could take her pain on himself. He knew firsthand just how badly it hurt.

"I-I can't believe I got shot."

"Here, let me see." Garrett gently probed the side she'd indicated and breathed a sigh of relief when he found the wound. "You lucked out, he only grazed you. In fact, we'll have matching scars."

She opened her eyes and met his gaze. "I want you to know how sorry I am. Ethan nearly died because of me."

"Ethan is *alive* because of you. My God, you took a bullet for him. Do you have any idea how grateful I am to you?" He smoothed a stray lock of hair away from her eyes.

"It's my fault he was in that situation in the first place. I don't know how you can stand to look at me."

The last was said in a near whisper. A tear slipped from the corner of her eyes and trailed down her cheek. Garrett wanted to take her in his arms and comfort her, but the whining of a siren grew deafeningly loud as an ambulance pulled up in front of her house.

He rose to his feet and stepped over to where Lyle lay motionless on the floor. Garrett knew he was dead, or damn close to it. While Garrett derived no pleasure from the man's death, he knew he wouldn't have any nightmares over it either. He was just glad to have the people he cared about safe and sound.

Jessica clamped down on her bottom lip as the paramedics cleansed and bandaged her wound. The bullet, they told her, had made quite a crease in her side, but thankfully, that was the extent of the damage. Another inch in and the bullet could have lodged between her ribs...or worse.

Do you have any idea how grateful I am to you? Garrett's words replayed over and over in her mind until she thought she might scream. Dammit, she didn't want his gratitude, she wanted...what the hell *did* she want? His heart? Fresh tears burned her eyes. Yep, his heart was exactly what she wanted, but not because he was grateful or felt obligated. She wanted him because he loved her. Nothing less could ever be enough.

Lord, she was tired. Not just physically, but mentally. She thought about Marky and was actually able to smile a bit. Jessica hadn't been able to save her son, but she had saved Ethan, and in some small way that freed her; made her feel whole again.

Made her feel worthy.

Garrett crouched down beside her. "Soon as you get a couple pain killers in you, you'll feel much better, I promise."

I love him so much. That old saying 'If you love something set it free' came to mind, and though it would just about kill her, Jessica knew she had no choice but to do exactly that.

She watched the paramedics check Wade from head to toe and rolled her eyes at his nonstop whining. My God, what had she ever seen in that man? The only good thing he'd ever done was help her create Marky. He hadn't even asked whether his own brother was dead or alive.

As they wheeled him past her toward the front door, Wade lifted his head and said, "So Jessie, now that you lost your waitressing job, what are you going to do? I hear they have some strip clubs over on the east side of town." He turned to Garrett. "Jessie's a stripper, did you know that? Gives the best lap dance you'll ever have and—"

Garrett shot across the room and grabbed Wade by the throat. It took two cops and three paramedics to pry him off. When Wade lie utterly still, Jessica feared Garrett had choked him to death.

Then her ex wheezed and coughed and rasped, "I...want that bastard...arrested! I'm pressing...charges this time, Jessie!"

The officers apologized to Garrett, then she watched in horror as they pulled his arms behind his back and cuffed him.

When Garrett offered no resistance, Jessica cried, "No, please, Wade goaded him! He doesn't deserve—"

"I'll be fine," Garrett said, his expression inscrutable. "Worry about yourself."

Her heart wrenched in her chest. He'd come to her defense because that's the kind of man he was—honorable. But she could've sworn she'd detected a flicker of disgust in his gaze, and Jessica died a little inside as she remembered his words. *"Not that I'm into strippers."*

"Well, where the hell is she?" Garrett strode out of the jail cell more pissed off than when he'd gone in. He'd spent three nights behind bars, and Jessica hadn't come to see him once. Okay, she'd been injured, he knew that. He hadn't given it a second thought when she hadn't shown up the first night. He hadn't batted an eyelash over the fact she hadn't called the station to check on him. But now, the look on his brother's face said it all.

Jessica was gone.

Nicky clapped him on the back. "Sorry, but we're not sure. Sara's been trying to call to see if she needs any help, but there's no answer. Her machine hasn't even picked up. And her truck's been gone since the night before last, best we can figure."

Garrett silently fumed as they hopped in Nicky's Jeep and headed home. As soon as they pulled up to the curb, he threw his door open and stormed up to Jessica's front door. Her truck was nowhere in sight and all the curtains were drawn.

"Hey, you mutant fur ball!" he called out, praying Mr. Louie would come running from around the back of the house. If her cat was here, Jess was here. She'd never leave him behind, of that Garrett was certain.

But Mr. Louie never came, and Garrett had to face facts.

Jessica had left him.

He spent the next week getting his life back in order. He spoke to his superior officer about coming back from his leave of absence as soon as the in-house investigation was over. Due to recent events, Garrett realized he loved being a cop and couldn't imagine a career in anything other than law enforcement. He also made a conscious decision to start looking for a place of his own. He was nearly thirty-two years old and still living at home, for crissakes.

Most importantly, he worked at letting go of the pipe dream that he and Jessica would live happily ever after. She must have wanted to get away from him pretty damn bad if she hadn't even waited for her wound to heal before starting the long drive back to Seattle.

Well, good riddance.

He deserved better than someone who was constantly yanking his chain.

Of course, it would help if her beautiful face didn't haunt him every time he closed his eyes.

Muriel lay naked and content in Luke's arms, this having been the first time they'd been alone since the awful incident at Jessica's house. She thanked God that everyone she cared about was all right. Well, Garrett had been moping around like a lost puppy since Charlie's niece had headed back home to Seattle. But only time would heal those wounds.

Luke's hand gently kneaded her hip; her fingers drew lazy circles on his chest. They'd just spent two of the most incredible hours of her life in bed, and she'd come close to tears as he'd loved her like no man ever had before.

Her ex-husband wasn't an evil guy, but he'd had a roving eye that could've put Casanova to shame. After the fourth affair, she'd decided enough was enough. Staying married for the sake of her kids wasn't good for any of them if she was miserable. So, she'd kicked his philandering butt out of the house and filed for divorce. Six years later, she bought the home she presently lived in, and although she'd dated plenty since, she hadn't felt anything more than a passing attraction for another man...until Luke.

"Muriel?"

"Hmmm?" Her hand stilled and she lifted her head to meet his gaze.

He cleared his throat twice—something he only did when he was especially nervous—and said, "I realize we haven't been dating that long and, well, I'm not exactly sure of the protocol, but..."

Another throat clearing, and Muriel reached up to stroke his beloved whiskery face.

Luke smiled and his eyes grew smoky with renewed desire. "I love you."

"Oh, Luke," Muriel threw her arms around his neck and squeezed her eyes shut to stem the flood of tears threatening to spill. "I love you, too. You've made me happier than I ever thought possible."

"Well, now, I'm not normally a betting man, but I think I can kick happy up a notch to delirious."

He started kneading the soft flesh of her backside, and she nipped at his ear in return. "There's not a doubt in my mind. But first, I have a proposition for you. Interested?"

"You know I am." He pressed the proof of his interest against her thigh.

She giggled. "Not what I had in mind, although that's a given. Luke? How would you feel about...moving in with me? I know we haven't been seeing each other very long, but...I don't know...it just feels right."

He tipped her face up and kissed her, a slow, lingering kiss that left her hungry for more. "Honey, I'd run home and pack my bags right now, 'cept I'm pretty sure I couldn't run in my condition."

Muriel laughed. "As much fun as that would be to watch, I don't plan to let you leave this bed anytime soon."

And she was nothing if not a woman of her word.

Fifteen

"I'm so glad you decided to come home."

Jessica forced a smile as her mother poured her a second cup of coffee. She glanced around the kitchen, trying to find comfort in the familiarity of home. The butter-yellow painted walls; her mother's collection of teapots, which graced every spare inch of space on her shelves and cupboards; the Last Supper picture which hung above the cherry antique pie safe her mother cherished.

"I never should've left."

Her mother reached across the table to grasp her hand. "I'm just grateful you're safe. I always knew Wade was a good for nothing bum, but I had no idea his brother was so unbalanced. Poor Lita."

Jessica silently concurred. She knew exactly how it felt to bury a son. Wade's mother, a good woman who'd unfortunately raised two bad seeds, didn't deserve the heartache she was suffering right now—burying one son, while her other faced a second prison term.

"He won't say it, but your father is happy you're home, too."

Jessica cocked a brow. She knew her father loved her, but their relationship had been strained since the day he discovered she'd been a stripper. And what made it worse was the way he'd found out: he and his bowling buddies had walked in on her act. Frankly, she thought his attitude a bit hypocritical considering. But he was her father, after all, so she'd kept her mouth shut while he'd read her the riot act.

"Mom, I'll need to earn a paycheck while I'm here. Can I have my old job back, or have you already replaced me?" She reached across the table for one of the fresh gingersnaps that were a specialty in her parents' coffee shop.

"While you're here?" her mother repeated. "Please tell me you're not considering going back. I couldn't take it if—"

"Relax, Mom. I meant here in your home. I'll want to move into my own place soon."

The thought of never seeing Garrett's handsome face again was unbearable. She wanted him, needed him...loved him. God, how she loved him. If only she'd met him before Wade...No, then she wouldn't have had her son, and she couldn't imagine her life without Marky in it, even for such a short time.

She lifted the gingersnap to her lips, but the spicy-sweet smell didn't mingle well with her stomach, and a wave of nausea caught her by surprise. She set the cookie on her saucer and swallowed hard.

"Jessie?" Her mother leaned forward and peered at her with those keen eyes. "You don't look so good. Are you feeling all right?"

"I'm fine, just tired. It was a long drive."

"You should've flown. It's a miracle that hunk-a-junk made it here."

Jessica couldn't hold back a small grin. "Are you

insulting my truck?"

With a roll of her eyes, her mother rose from the table and carried her cup to the sink. "That truck—and I use the term loosely—should have gone to the big junkyard in the sky years ago."

Before Jessica could respond, the back door opened and her father stepped into the kitchen. It felt as if all the air got sucked out of the room, and she struggled to take a breath. "Hi, Daddy."

"Thought I recognized that accident on wheels."

A surprisingly uncertain smile lifted the corners of her father's mouth, and Jessica was caught off guard by a flood of emotion. Tears burned the backs of her eyes and her lips quivered. Damn, when had she become such an emotional basket case?

"Jessica, give your father a kiss. Ed, can I make you a sandwich? I picked up some nice rare roast beef and crusty hard rolls from the deli."

He walked over and held out his arms. Jessica flew into them with a relieved sob. Things had been strained between them for so long, and it was such a comfort to have her daddy back again. The one who didn't judge her, or make her feel lower than dirt.

"It's good to have you home, kitten." He kissed her on the forehead, then took the seat beside her. "A roast beef sandwich sounds great, Mare, thanks." He reached out and chucked Jessica under the chin. "Join me?"

Her stomach flipped at the thought. "Thanks, but I think I'll go take a nap. I'm beat."

"You should've flown," he gently admonished.

"So I've been told." She rose to her feet. "But then I would've had to leave Mr. Louie in Green Bay, and there's no way I could've done that."

Her father glanced around in feigned dismay. "I almost forgot about that mountain lion you call a cat. Mare, make sure that thing doesn't steal my sandwich."

"I'll protect it with my life," her mother said with a playful roll of her eyes. She walked over and set his plate on the table, earning a pat on the backside.

"Well, that's my cue," Jessica teased. "See you at supper."

"Son, you have to go after her."

"Like hell." Garrett didn't spare his uncle even a quick glance.

"Look,"—the older man let out a huff of exasperation—"we all do things sometimes we're not proud of, but—"

Garrett shot to his feet and tossed the hammer aside. He'd been putting the finishing touches on Ethan's doghouse when Uncle Luke approached. Christ, why couldn't they all just leave him the hell alone?

"How can you even defend her after what she did? Why can't any of you look at it from my point of view?" He stormed into the house and headed for the fridge. His uncle followed him inside.

"Because we love you. And you love her, even if you're too pig-headed to admit it."

"Hmmph." Garrett poured himself a glass of iced tea, then leaned back against the counter, crossing his feet at the ankles as he eyed the black clouds rolling in. He wanted to get that doghouse finished before the storm hit. Mike and Sara planned to take Ethan to the Humane Society tomorrow to pick out a puppy and—

"Ignoring me isn't going to make this go away. You deserve to be happy, son, and that girl makes you happy. So she...danced for a little while. I'm sure she had a good reason, like keeping a roof over her and her son's head and food in their bellies. And a minimum wage job just don't—"

"What the hell are you talking about? You think I'm pissed off because she was a stripper?" He pushed to the back of his mind the fact that his own unknowing comment weeks ago was probably the reason she'd never confided in him about her past profession.

Uncle Luke's brow furrowed. "What else?"

Garrett straightened and set his glass on the counter with more force than necessary. "How about the fact that she left town without so much as a goodbye? I sat in a jail cell for three nights, and she never even stopped in to see me, to let me know she was all right."

"She was devastated. And no doubt shamed out of her skin. That ex of hers not only wreaked havoc on all of us, he ripped open wounds of hers that were still fresh. His brother damn near raped Muriel, he shot at Ethan. And I don't need to remind you who took the bullet for him."

With a muttered curse, Garrett swiped up his iced tea and gulped half of it down.

Uncle Luke strode across the kitchen and poured himself a cup of coffee. He sat down at the table and added, "If it's your pride holding you back, then get over it. We're all human, son. We don't always make the best decisions. Just look at all the time Sara and Mike lost."

Garrett exhaled a heavy sigh. "Look, I know you mean well, but it's time to face facts. Jessica and I just weren't meant to be. I know it, she knows it, and I think deep down, you know it, too."

Uncle Luke gave his head a sad shake. "The only thing I know for sure is you're making the biggest mistake of your life."

"Glad to see you got your appetite back."

Jessica scooped a second helping of her mother's baked chicken and rice casserole onto her plate, then snitched a third corn muffin from the napkin-lined basket and slathered it with butter. "What can I say? I've missed your cooking." She suspected it was more than that, but there was no sense in worrying about it now. She had at least a couple more months before her mother's eagle eye outed her.

"You've loved this dish since you were a little girl."

Jessica looked up and caught her parents sharing an odd glance. Her heart skipped a beat and her hand paused halfway to her mouth. My God, did they already suspect her secret? *Calm down*, she silently scolded herself. They couldn't possibly know. Heck, *she* didn't even know for sure. It was just a gut feeling she had. Well, that and the fact she could barely stand the smell of her favorite cookies. With Marky, it had been her fabric softener, and she'd had to switch brands until her third trimester.

She happened to catch another strange look pass between her parents and decided enough was enough. She set her fork down with a clink. "All right, what is it?"

Her mother's wide-eyed innocent look was less than convincing. Her father's reluctance to speak was just as telling.

"I'm a big girl, you know. I can handle whatever it

is."

Her father raked his fingers through his hair, then started drumming them on the table.

Her mother frowned, and he stopped. They both waited for the other to speak. Finally, her mother said, "Lita stopped by while you were resting."

Jessica closed her eyes and rubbed them with her thumb and forefinger. No way was she ready to face her ex-mother-in-law. Lita Hastings had treated her well at one time, but there'd certainly been hard feelings after Wade went to prison. Jessica hadn't spoken on his behalf at the sentencing trial, and she knew Lita probably hadn't forgiven her. Not completely anyway. And now here he was, facing prison time again while his brother lay in a fresh grave.

"What did she want?"

With a disgusted shake of his head, her father continued eating his supper.

"She...she doesn't want you to testify against Wade. She said you've cost her enough and owe her at least that much."

Jessica stared at her parents, willing back the tears. As a mother herself, she couldn't blame Lita for wanting to save her one remaining child from more prison time. But how could she do that to Garrett? He'd also been through the wringer because of her. The dull throbbing in her side reminded her of just how much more he could have lost...because of her.

My God, she was a jinx. A tear slid from the corner of her eye, then another.

With a muttered curse, her father tossed down his fork, which clattered off his plate and onto the linoleum floor. "Nothing that happened was your fault, do you hear me? You moved halfway across the country to start a new life, and that idiot chased after you. You have no control over what other people do. And you *will* testify against him. He should've never been let out in the first place, that irresponsible, son of a—"

"Ed, please," her mother cried. "The last thing she needs in her condition is you hollering at her."

Startled, Jessica's gaze flew to her mother's face. The older lady composed herself, cleared her throat and amended, "It's barely been a week since she was shot."

Her father scowled, took a deep breath, then gulped back the rest of his soda. "I think I'll run down to the shop, get the inventory started."

As soon as the door slammed behind him, her mother said, "I agree with him, you know. I feel for Lita, I truly do, but if Wade goes free, you'll be looking over your shoulder for the rest of your life."

Jessica swiped at her eyes. Of course, her parents were right. What kind of life would she have if she was constantly waiting for Wade to show up and turn her world upside down—again? Not to mention the guilt that would eat at her soul if she let him get away with what he'd done. Lyle may have been the one who attacked Muriel, held a gun to Ethan's head, and shot her, but Wade was just as guilty as if he'd pulled the trigger himself.

He'd stolen an estimated eight hundred and sixty thousand dollars-worth of diamond rings from Lennox Jewelers, too. Jessica still couldn't quite believe that one. She remembered the news stories, remembered the rings had never been recovered and no suspects ever found. But never in a million years would Jessica have suspected her own husband and his bumbling brother had been responsible.

And Wade no doubt expected her to be his alibi, to swear Lyle had been solely responsible for stealing the rings. Jessica glanced into the living room to the eight by ten photograph that hung above her parents' wedding picture. Marky, grinning into the camera, blue eyes so full of life, his little bear clutched in his fist, as always. With complete clarity, Jessica knew she had no choice. Wade wouldn't walk away with a slap on the wrist this time.

***

"So, are you home to stay, young lady?"

Jessica poured Mr. Delmarco a cup of coffee and forced a smile. The sweet old man, who worked in the meat market across the street, had been coming into her parents' coffee shop since the day it opened. "I sure am. It's like Dorothy said in *The Wizard of Oz*. 'There's no place like home.'"

"Atta girl."

"Now, what can I get you? The blueberry scones just came out of the oven," she said with a tempting lilt to her voice.

Mr. Delmarco's faded blue eyes lit up. "Bring me two."

Jessica had just set the plate down in front of him when a hush fell over the shop. She looked up in time to see Lita Hastings step inside, her gaze immediately zeroing in on Jessica. Her shoulder-length, graying blonde hair looked like it hadn't seen a brush in days, and even from across the room, Jessica could read the desolation in the older woman's dark brown eyes.

She walked past Jessica and headed toward a booth in the back of the shop. Ignoring the murmurs, Jessica steeled her resolve, took a deep breath, and followed in her ex-mother-in-law's wake. She slid into the booth across from her.

"You have to know how sorry I am about Lyle. But Wade—"

Lita gave her head a vehement shake, the hate in her eyes unmistakable. The kind lady Jessica had known since grade school had been replaced by a bitter woman who had nothing else to live for if she lost her sole remaining child to another prison term. A much longer prison term this time now that he had a criminal record.

"I don't care how sorry you are. In fact, I don't care about you at all. I lost my grandson because of you. I lost my son because of you. And now Wade's facing twenty to life, because of *you*. Save your apologies and do the right thing. Keep Wade from going to prison again, and save me from losing the only person left in my life I care about. You owe me that much."

Jessica just barely kept her composure. "I understand why you blame me for...everything. But deep down, you know I'm no more responsible for their actions than you are."

Lita's eyes widened, and she drew back as if she'd been slapped. "How dare you!" She pursed her lips, glanced around, and then lowered her voice. "To even suggest I'm to blame."

"That's not what I said, or what I meant." Jessica blinked back tears. She reached across the table and clasped the older woman's hand. "Lita, come on. Wade and Lyle were always on the wild side, you know that. They both had juvy records long before I met them."

Her ex-mother-in-law snatched her hand back as if burned. Her eyes grew cold. "This coming from a girl who shed her clothes for money—and Lord only knows what else?"

Jessica's anger finally surfaced. "I had no choice, and you know it. Wade couldn't keep a job to save his life. The rent was a month late. The electric was going to be shut off any day, and I had a child to think about. Dancing was the only job I could get that paid cash, and paid me every night."

"Dancing," Lita sneered. "Listen, you can call it what you want, but you took off your clothes for money, which is no better than a prostitute in my book. Now—"

"Get the hell out of my shop, Lita."

Jessica looked up in surprise at her father's quietly spoken command. She hadn't even heard him approach.

The woman shot him a scathing look, snatched her purse off the table, and rose to her feet. "Jessica, if you testify against Wade, against your own son's father...may God have mercy on your soul."

"Miserable woman," her father muttered as she stalked away. "And a hypocrite, too. I haven't seen Lita in church since..."

"Since Marky's funeral?" Jessica finished for him, meeting his gaze.

He let out a frustrated breath. "Honey, why don't you go upstairs and lie down? You look a little...peaked."

It was on the tip of her tongue to argue with him, but the truth was, she didn't feel all that well, and a nap sounded heavenly. "Thanks, Daddy."

By the time Jessica woke up from her nap, the sun was nothing but a golden blanket over the western horizon.

She rolled over and squinted at the clock. *Holy cow.* She'd slept for over five hours! Why hadn't her parents woken her up?

Jessica sat up and a wave of nausea hit her with the force of a gale wind. She took a deep breath, waited for it to pass, then slowly stood and headed into the bathroom. After a nice, hot shower, she felt much better and followed her nose down to the kitchen as hunger pains gripped her. A foil-covered pan sat on the stove, and she nearly squealed with delight when she uncovered lasagna. And sure enough, a basket with still-warm breadsticks sat on the counter beside it.

She pulled a plate and fork from the dishwasher, then grabbed a spatula out of the utensil drawer and cut herself a hunk. Then she dug around in the fridge for the parmesan cheese.

When she swung the door shut, Garrett was standing there, hands on hips, brow creased, his expression unfathomable.

Jessica shrieked and fell backward against the kitchen table as the container of cheese flew into the air.

He caught the parmesan with one hand and grasped her arm with the other to steady her. "Jesus, I didn't mean to scare you. Are you all right?"

She took several deep breaths and pulled her arm from his grasp. He looked so handsome it nearly took her breath away. "Wh-what are you doing here?"

He crossed his arms and cocked a brow. "You certainly know how to make a man feel welcome."

Jessica saw a shadow move behind him before her

Meant To Be

parents stepped into the room. Her dad clapped Garrett on the back, and her mother actually beamed up at him. Jessica resisted the urge to roll her eyes. Heck, the truth was, she knew exactly how her mother felt. Garrett, dressed in a slightly worn pair of jeans and a royal blue collared shirt, looked like he'd just stepped off the cover of a magazine.

"Officer Jamison came all the way from Green Bay to see you," her mother needlessly pointed out.

"Thanks, Mom, but I managed to figure that out all by myself."

Garrett frowned at her. "Don't sass your mother. That's disrespectful."

Her mother twittered—actually *twittered!*

"Thank you, Officer. Jessie's a good girl, but she does tend to get a bit mouthy."

"Please, call me Garrett."

"Garrett," her mother repeated a little breathlessly.

Finally, Jessica's father wrapped his arm around her mother and said, "Come on, Mary, we'd better let these two talk. Garrett, it was a pleasure to meet you."

"You, too, sir. Ma'am."

Jessica waited 'til they were out of earshot before muttering, "Jackass."

Garrett laughed. "Man, I thought it was just mornings, but you're crabby no matter what time you wake up. And aren't you a little old for an afternoon nap?" He walked over to the stove and peeked under the foil. "Lasagna? Damn, that smells good. Would you mind heating me up some, too? Thanks."

He strode over and took a seat at the kitchen table, leaned back and kicked his feet up on the chair next to his. Jessica took a couple of deep breaths to compose herself. She opened the dishwasher to retrieve another plate and fork, then cut the arrogant jerk a huge slice of lasagna.

They ate in silence, the only sound to break it was the clinking of forks on plates. After scraping his clean, Garrett wiped his mouth on a paper napkin, stretched his arms over his head, and let out a deep, masculine groan. "Don't suppose you have something for dessert?"

Jessica glared at him. "Get it yourself. What do I look like, your maid?"

With a chuckle, he rose to his feet and headed straight for the cake dome on the counter. He let out a low whistle when he uncovered the German chocolate cake beneath. "It's a miracle your father's as slim as he is," he commented as he scooped up a finger full of coconut-pecan frosting.

Scowling, Jessica set her fork on her plate and crossed her arms over her chest. "Fast metabolisms run in the family."

Garrett searched through the cupboards till he came across the small plates. "Good to know. Can I cut you a slice of cake, Miss Crabbypants?"

She pushed back from the table and shot to her feet. All at once, the room started spinning, and she had to grab the back of the chair for support. Unfortunately, the lasagna and breadsticks she'd eaten decided to wage war with her stomach, and her stomach seemed to be winning the battle. She took several deep breaths in an effort to calm things down.

"Hey, are you all right?" Garrett raced to her side. "You don't look so—Jesus!"

He jumped back, but it was too late as Jessica puked all over his shoes.

Sixteen

"Jessie, you have to tell him," her mother insisted. "He'll marry you, I'm sure of it."

Lying on her bed staring at the ceiling, Jessica wasn't sure whether to laugh or cry...or both. Of course Garrett would marry her. The man was as honorable as the day was long. But she'd already married once due to an unplanned pregnancy, and look how well that had turned out. She couldn't bear to see whatever affection Garrett had for her fade from his eyes as he grew to resent her for trapping him into marriage.

On the other hand, he had a right to know. He may not love her, but he would love his child with everything he had, of that she had no doubt. Shared custody would be a little difficult with them living so far apart, but they could make it work...somehow.

"He must love you very much. He came all this way just to see you."

Jessica rolled onto her side and closed her eyes. After utterly humiliating herself by gacking all over his shoes, she'd raced upstairs, sobbing, her mother right behind her. Now, Garrett and her father were having a beer down in the living room while her mother tried to coax her out of the bedroom. It wasn't exactly easy to face someone after you'd spewed all over them. And of course, he'd want to know why...

"Jessie, please talk to me."

Okay, he had come all this way just to see her, and since he couldn't possibly have known she was pregnant, maybe he *had* come after her. Maybe he truly did love her and meant to take her back home.

Home? But Seattle was her home. At least, it had been, until she'd fallen in love with the city of Green Bay...and with her hardheaded neighbor. A dull pounding started in the back of her skull, and she bit back a groan as she sat up.

"I'm okay. I just need to think. I mean, I've been down this road before, Mom, and we both know how it ended. Who's to say this time will be any different?"

"Who's to say it won't? Honey, of course there are no guarantees. Life doesn't work that way. But you've made mistakes and learned from them. And let's face it, Garrett Jamison is nothing like Wade. He'd take care of you, Jessie. Provide for you so you wouldn't have to go out and—"

"And strip for cash?" Jessica could hear the bitterness in her own voice.

Her mother frowned and shook her head. "I was going to say 'get a job.' You have to quit beating yourself up. You did what you had to do."

"Dad didn't seem to think so."

Her mother let out a delicate snort. "Your father was more embarrassed that he'd gotten caught in a strip club than anything else, trust me."

Jessica blew out a heavy breath. She sat up and swung her legs over the side of the bed. "Well, I'd best go get this over with before Garrett drinks Dad into a coma."

"Can I get you another?"

Garrett handed Jessica's father his empty beer bottle and shook his head. "Thanks, but I need to get up early tomorrow. And I have to drive to the hotel yet tonight."

Ed McGovern carried the empties into the kitchen. When he returned he said, "Nonsense, you can stay here. We have three guest rooms on the third floor."

Garrett glanced up from the ball game on TV. "I appreciate the offer, sir, but I have a feeling Jessica wouldn't take it so well. In case you hadn't noticed, she's not exactly happy to see me."

Ed waved that off. "Women. You know how they get. All that hormone stuff going on. Don't worry, though, it'll only last another month or—"

"Ed, can I see you in the kitchen?"

Garrett looked up, surprised to see Jessica and her mother standing at the foot of the stairs. He hadn't even heard them come down.

Jessica looked better, he noticed; her color had returned. July was an odd time to pick up a bug, but stranger things had happened. She seemed reluctant to make eye contact with him, and Garrett's heart softened a bit. Not like she was the first woman to puke on him. Sara had when she was pregnant with...Ethan. Garrett swallowed—hard. Jesus, it couldn't be...could it?

"Women. You know how they get? All that hormone stuff going on. Don't worry, though, it'll only last another month or—"

Garrett's gaze dropped to Jessica's stomach, but he quickly realized she wouldn't be far enough along to show yet. He rose to his feet, grateful when his knees

233

didn't buckle. Hell, this was what he'd hoped for, what he'd wanted more than anything. But did Jessica? So much had happened since the night they'd made love.

Another thought occurred to him. If she *was* pregnant, did she intend to tell him? His blood ran cold at the thought that she didn't.

Her father rushed over and smiled at his scowling wife. Garrett crossed his arms over his chest and watched as the three of them exchanged odd looks and hushed whispers. Jessica finally met his gaze as her mother dragged her father into the kitchen. He could hear more furious whispering, and his suspicions grew.

"So," Jessica said, stepping into the living room, "I never did ask, what brings you to Seattle?"

You, you exasperating woman. "I'm meeting with the DA tomorrow to go over my testimony regarding the stolen rings."

"Oh. Of course." She walked past him and curled up in the corner of the couch.

Garrett took a seat on the opposite end. She looked tired, and he wanted nothing more than to take her in his arms and soothe the worry from her brow. Even in a pair of sweats and a faded blue T-shirt, her honey-blonde hair pulled up in a hairclip, the woman was stunning.

Christ, you got it bad.

They watched the ball game for maybe five minutes before he finally admitted, "I've missed you."

Jessica turned to look at him, clearly surprised. "I don't know how you could after...Ethan almost got shot because of me. And Muriel..." She swung her attention back to the TV. He realized she was crying when she reached up to swipe away a tear.

With a muttered curse, Garrett slid over and crushed

her in his arms. Jessica resisted for all of five seconds before wrapping her arms around his neck and weeping softly. He hated that she blamed herself for what had happened.

The thought that his child could be growing inside her made his chest ache in a way he'd never experienced before. He had secretly yearned for a family of his own for years. He'd put it off, though, careful not to become seriously involved with anyone because Sara and Ethan had needed him. But not anymore, and if he was being truthful with himself, he knew no other woman would ever do for him. The thought that Jessica might not feel the same way scared the hell out of him.

"Nothing that happened was your fault, do you hear me? You are *not* responsible for your ex-husband's crimes. You had no idea he'd hidden stolen jewelry in your son's toy, and you had no way of knowing that scumbag Lyle would attack Muriel, or take aim at Ethan."

She coughed, sniffled, and wiped her eyes on the hem of her T-shirt. "If I'd just told you the truth from the beginning, none of it would've happened. But I was embarrassed I'd married such a loser, and ashamed...but I did what I had to do," she insisted, the fire back in her voice. "The bills were piling up, the rent was due, the utilities were all months behind. And Wade didn't care. All he wanted to do was suck down beer, watch TV, and screw the neighbor."

He kissed the top of her head. "Sweetheart, you don't owe me any explanations."

"Yes, I do. I brought those nutcases into your life, into your family's lives."

How ironic. Garrett had recently apologized to his

family for the same exact thing. If anyone knew how Jessica felt, he did.

"If I'd have just packed Marky up and moved back in with my parents," she continued, her voice an anguished whisper, "he'd still be alive. My son is dead because of my foolish pride."

He tightened his arms around her. "Sweetheart, your son's death was *not* your fault. It was an accident, a horrible accident. If anyone's to blame, it's his father. He should've been watching him, plain and simple. Wade failed Marky, and he failed you, too."

"I don't know why you're being so nice to me. I-I ran out of town like a coward. I couldn't face you. I couldn't face anyone."

He tipped her face up, forcing her to meet his gaze. "I was angry, believe me. I convinced myself you didn't give a damn about me."

She frowned, and he leaned down to press his lips to her wrinkled forehead. With a sigh, she snuggled in his arms.

"How's Jack?"

Garrett froze. *Jack?* She's thinking about that idiot at a time like this? He released her, sat up, and swiped his fingers through his hair. "He's fine. Mentioned heading down to some small town in central Illinois. Thinks he may have some relatives there." Garrett would choke before letting his jealousy show.

Her brow furrowed again, and she cast him a curious look before curling back up in the corner of the couch. "Oh."

Oh? Was that disappointment he detected in her tone? Jesus, she was carrying *his* kid, yet thinking about another man? Frustrated, he blew out a heavy breath and rose to his feet. "I think I'd better head to the hotel. I still need to check in."

She met his gaze again, arms crossed, uncertainty and an emotion he couldn't name reflected in her eyes. She'd withdrawn into herself, and Garrett was torn between wanting to crush her in his arms again or shake some sense into her. They belonged together, dammit. Why couldn't she see that? Sutton couldn't make her happy. Sutton didn't love her...

But I do. God help him, he loved the infuriating woman more than he'd ever thought possible.

"Will I see you again before you leave?" she said.

Garrett's pulse picked up speed. My God, she planned to let him walk out of her parents' home—out of her life!—without a single word of protest? "Do you want to?"

Her eyes widened and he felt a glimmer of hope. "I... Sure, if you have time. I don't want to put you out, but...I'm sure my parents will want to say goodbye."

Her parents? Her only concern was whether or not her parents got a chance to say goodbye? Jesus, the woman was certifiable! She was very probably carrying his child, yet had no intention, it seemed, to tell him. The thought was inconceivable.

Angry, confused, heartbroken, he spun around and strode toward the front door.

"Garrett?"

He stopped, hand on the doorknob, heart pounding furiously against his ribcage. "Yeah?"

"I..." She cleared her throat. "If you don't have time to stop back tomorrow, have a safe trip home."

Garrett squeezed his eyes shut, opened the door, and walked out of her life.

Jessica's knees gave out as the echo of the slammed door reverberated throughout the room. Unable to hold back the tears, she collapsed onto the hardwood floor and sobbed her heart out.

He'd left her. It was over. She'd wanted to tell him about the baby, had been on the verge of blurting it out. But standing at the door, his back to her, his hand on the knob as if he couldn't get out of there fast enough, the words got stuck in her throat. She knew she'd have to tell him eventually. The man had a right to know he'd fathered a child. But she could wait now. Give him some time to get his life and career back on track before—

The front door swung open and there he stood, hands on hips, jaw working furiously as he pinned her to the floor with his steely-eyed gaze.

"I can't friggin' believe you let me walk out of here without telling me you're pregnant."

He shut the door and strode forward, reaching down to help her to her feet. Jessica stared up at him, stunned. *He knows? But...how?* Her father swore he hadn't told him—

"Don't you dare try to deny it either. All the pieces fit."

She slowly shook her head. Out of her peripheral vision she saw her father start toward them, and her mother pull him back by his shirt collar. The ridiculousness of it caused a bubble of laughter to escape. She bit her bottom lip as Garrett's frown turned into a full-blown scowl.

"You think this is funny? Christ, Jess, is it all just a game to you? This is my child we're talking about."

Damn the man and his detective skills. She scowled right back. "I don't think this is the least bit funny, you jackass. And I *had* planned to tell you about the baby, I was just waiting for the right time."

"Yeah? When would that be, when he was graduating from college?"

She poked him in the chest. "How do you go from hero to jerk in such a short period of time? And what makes you think it's a boy? There's just as much chance we'll have a little girl."

That announcement seemed to take the wind from his sails. He grew a little green around the gills as he dropped down onto the taupe leather armchair in the corner. "Of course...a little girl. And she'll look just like you, which means I'll never get another night's sleep for as long as I live."

Now, there was a half-ass compliment if she'd ever heard one. Jessica strode over and knelt beside him. She grinned. "I doubt it'll be that bad."

A reluctant smile chased away his frown. He reached out and cupped her cheek. "I want this baby, Jessica. And I want you. I'm so in love with you I can barely see straight."

Her heart swelled. She leaned into his hand as tears filled her eyes. "And I love you, you annoying, wonderful man."

A choked sob sounded behind them, and they both spun around. Her parents stood arm in arm, her mother leaning into her father for support, a smile as bright as the noon sun lighting up her face. Her father sent Garrett an approving nod.

"Come on, Mary," he said, "let's give these kids some privacy." With a gentle nudge, he escorted her back into the kitchen.

Garrett chuckled. He stood up and took Jessica into

his arms. She gazed up, happier than she'd been in years. It was hard to fathom that her life had come full circle, only this time, she had no doubt she'd get the happy ending she'd always dreamed of. Oh, it would be a long and bumpy ride for sure. But when you had love on your side, anything was possible.

Garrett leaned back and reached into his front pants pocket. When he pulled out a small velvet box, Jessica gasped and started dancing in place. He laughed.

"Is that...is that what I think it is?" she breathed, wanting to snatch it from his hand and crack the sucker open herself.

"This,"—he opened the beautiful blue box, and the most stunning diamond ring she'd ever seen sparkled up at her—"is the real reason I came to Seattle."

She looked in absolute wonder. "But you said—"

"That I had to go over my testimony with the DA? Heck, I could have done that over the phone."

Hope blossomed in her chest. "So...you came for *me*?"

"I came for you," he confirmed, love shining from his eyes.

Then he dropped to one knee and clasped her left hand.

Jessica's squeal of delight mingled with a second—much louder—squeal from behind her. She twisted around to smile at her mother through her tears. "I knew daddy wouldn't be able to keep you away."

Garrett waved her parents forward. "May as well do this right," he said meeting her father's gaze. "Sir, I love your daughter. I promise to take care of her, provide for her, and keep her blissfully happy for the rest of her life. May I please have her hand in marriage?"

Her mother hooked an arm around Jessica's shoulders and kissed her on the cheek, while her father clasped her other hand. "Son, it would be my pleasure. Uncle Charlie's been talking you up for years. It's nice to see the old geezer was right about something."

"Ed!"

Garrett grinned. "He's a great old guy...but he does tell a lot of tall tales."

Jessica giggled and her mother gave her a playful pinch on the arm.

Garrett returned his attention to Jessica. He pulled the ring from the box and held it up for her parents to see. "Jessica, please put me out of my misery and say you'll marry me."

"I'll marry you, but on one condition."

He cocked a brow and eyed both her parents curiously, as if looking for a clue. "I'm listening."

"Promise me you'll never make another nasty remark about Tom Cruise."

Garrett grinned from ear to ear. "You drive a hard bargain, sweetheart, but it's a deal."

Epilogue

"Now, close your eyes and no peeking," Garrett said as he reached over Jessica and pulled open the nightstand drawer.

Eyes squeezed tightly shut, she smiled with delight as her body cooled down from the incredible hour they'd just spent making love. She slid up to lean against the pillow and caught her bottom lip between her teeth, anxious to know what the wonderful man had for her now. He placed what felt like papers in her hand.

"Go ahead, take a look."

Jessica opened her eyes, unsure of what she held. They widened and misted over when she realized she held the deed to Uncle Charlie's house in her hand. She looked up and met Garrett's gaze, her mouth open in shock.

He reached out and closed her mouth. "You'll draw flies," he teased as he snuggled her against his side.

Mr. Louie chose that moment to race into the room. He jumped up on the bed and sprawled out between them.

"But...how did you manage this?" Jessica reached over with her free hand to stroke between Mr. Louie's ears. "Uncle Charlie loves this house."

"He's an old man, Jess, with no kids or grandkids. He wants to spend the rest of his years traveling the world. He gave us a great deal, too," he added, rubbing her rounded belly.

"Well, that's a good thing since it looks like our diaper bills are going to be double what we'd figured." Jessica waited with bated breath for her words to sink in.

Garrett beamed as understanding dawned, and he let out a whoop so loud Mr. Louie jumped two feet in the air.

Grinning, Jessica reached up to stroke Garrett's beloved, stubbly face. She glanced at the dresser where a precious little brown bear sat, watching over all of them.

I love you, Marky. Watch over your brother and sister for us, too.

Author's Note:

I hope you enjoyed Garrett & Jessica's story. As soon as I finished writing *There's Only Been You* , I knew Garrett had to have a happily-ever-after of his own. Next up, Nick Jamison is much too serious for his own good.

And if you'd like to know how Danny & Emily found their own HEA, please check out FOOLISH PRIDE...

Foolish Pride

Jamison Series: Extra Peek Short Story

(Available wherever e-books are sold)

Youngest brother Danny Jamison has a lot to learn about women, and even more to learn about himself...

When God was handing out pride, Danny Jamison must have gotten in line twice, because he's about to let the best thing that's ever happened to him slip away—Emily Harris.

Emily is head-over-heels in love with Danny, but she's not sure she can take his jealous mood swings anymore. Something has to give or his Foolish Pride is going to be the end of them.

Sinking down until submersed to her neck, Emily bent her knees and closed her eyes, letting the steaming water work its magic. It seeped into her bones, relaxing her from head to toe as her worries seemed to melt away.

By feel alone, she grabbed her two-in-one shampoo, squeezed a small amount onto her head, and scrubbed like a mad woman. Once rinsed, she reached for the washcloth and bar of soap. She lathered up her face first, washing away her dried tears and every trace of make-up. She ran the washcloth over her shoulders, under her armpits, over her breasts and stomach. She moved the washcloth between her legs—

"I'd be more than happy to take over for you."

Emily squealed and sat up in a rush, splashing water all over the floor. When she realized it was Danny leaning against the doorframe, she threw the wet washcloth at him. "Dammit, you scared me half to death!"

He pushed away from the door and strode forward. "Sorry. I knocked, but you had Metallica blaring so loud you couldn't hear me."

"I find Metallica extremely relaxing!" she snapped. "Now give me back my key and get the hell out of my apartment." She held out her hand.

Danny knelt beside the tub, but instead of handing her the key he brushed his knuckles down her cheek. "Look, Em, I know you're royally pissed at me right now, but if you'd just give me a chance to explain, I—"

"Are you kidding me? 'Royally pissed' doesn't even begin to describe how I feel." Suddenly more angry than upset, she crossed her arms over her breasts and brought her knees up in an effort to preserve a little modesty. Which she knew was ridiculous since they'd been sleeping together for more than a year.

"You have no idea how sorry I am for what I said. It

was completely inexcusable. But...if you could just give me one more chance..." He grabbed her hand and brought it to his lips, holding it against his cheek as he said, his voice raw with emotion, "Em, I love you. And I know you love me, too."

Her eyes filled with tears. Damn him! Now? He waits until things are over between them to finally say those three little words she'd been waiting so patiently to hear him say? But...as much as she wanted to believe him, she couldn't, she just couldn't.

She jerked her hand from his. "I'm sorry, too, Danny, but I can't do this anymore. Your jealousy has gotten crazy lately and that temper...sometimes I'm afraid..."

Shock twisted his face into a mask of incredulity. "My God, I would never hurt you. How could you even think—"

"I don't know! That's the problem. It's like I have no idea who you are anymore. You're angry all the time, you've become so possessive." She reached up to swipe at her eyes. "It seems like the only time you're in a good mood anymore is when we're in bed."

"Then let's crawl in bed right now and stay there forever."

"Danny, please, just go. I can't do this right now. *Please.*"

With a deep sigh, he pushed to his feet, head hung low, and turned to leave. Looking back over his shoulder, he said, "Fine, I'll leave. Give you a couple days to get over your anger. But eventually we're going to talk about this. Because there's no way in hell I'm just going to just let you go."

Also by Donna Marie Rogers

GOLDEN OPPORTUNITY

Golden Series: Book 1

(Available wherever e-books are sold)

"Deliciously sweet...with plenty of heat!"
~ Norah Wilson,
New Voice In Romance award-winning author

James McMillan is a third generation owner of the most prosperous horse ranch in Golden, Colorado. When a gorgeous little filly shows up at his door waving what she claims is the deed to half his ranch, James tries to send her packing. But the document is authentic, according to his lawyer: Reese McMillan sold the little opportunist his half of the Double M during a poker game in Atlantic City. So not only must James find a way to buy those shares back, he needs to fight his growing attraction to his luscious new business partner—who turns out to be a lot more than just a pretty face.

Angela Roberts, having been on her own since she was a teenager, has never wanted anything more than the security of a real home. Her dreams come true when the chance to own half of a Colorado horse ranch falls into her lap. If Reese McMillan is too blind to appreciate what he has, that's his loss. Only she hadn't counted on the hostile reception she receives from his brother. Surly as a bear, James McMillan is also much too handsome for her peace of mind. Refusing to be intimidated, Angela sets out to win him over by proving she has what it takes to help him run the ranch—and ends up losing her heart to both.

One

"I'm telling you I bought it fair and square. This deed proves it."

James McMillan glared down at the crazy woman waving a document under his nose. So his fool baby brother had finally done it—he'd gambled away his half of the ranch. James' biggest fear had come true, and she barely reached his shoulder.

He blew out a silent breath and thumbed his Stetson back. "Look, Miss...?"

"Roberts. Angela Roberts."

"It'll take me a few days to raise the funds to buy it back. In the meantime, there are several hotels in downtown Golden—"

"Sorry, Cowboy, but you're not getting rid of me that easily. I'm staying right here at the Double M. Reese said—"

"Reese is an idiot, and I don't give a damn what he said. I'll be dipped if some gold-digging opportunist is gonna set one foot inside the home my great-grandparents built with their own hands. Now, I'll pay for your hotel room if you can't afford one, but either way, you're leaving."

She huffed out a sigh of frustration and crossed her arms over her ample chest. Big blue eyes clear as the Colorado sky gazed up at him, and for a brief moment, James became lost in them. He gave himself a mental shake, ignoring her full pouty lips and shiny auburn hair, which hung in loose waves down to her waist. Lord, did he love long hair on a woman.

Damn you, Reese.

"I told you, I'm not going anywhere. I own half this ranch, whether you like it or not. And if you insist on making me leave, I promise you I'll be back with the sheriff."

Great. Just freakin' great. Sheriff Martin would pounce like a mountain lion on a chance to make James miserable. And if she got that vindictive old cuss involved, the story of Reese's stupidity would be all over town by nightfall.

His frustration must have shown on his face because a knowing smile curved those luscious lips. James propped his hands on his hips in defeat and took a step back. "Fine. You wanna play house, lady, be my guest. Just don't get too comfortable."

With a toss of her head, she picked up her suitcase, her high heels clicking on the tiled floor of the foyer as she strode past him. It took all James' self-control not to give her denim-clad ass a swat as she passed by.

Angela gazed around the surprisingly modern log ranch house, nearly overcome by emotion. Her heart swelled with hope as she took in the vaulted ceiling, large stone fireplace, and overall rustic charm. So beautiful...and by being in the right place at the right time she was now half-owner. Reese had said the place was nothing special. Big brother was right about one thing; Reese was an idiot.

She turned to face Mr. Tall, Dark, and Incredibly Handsome, feeling a sudden pang of insecurity. "I've never seen a more beautiful home. Reese made it sound...well, I didn't know what to expect."

"Reese always preferred bright lights and the big city over the hard work of running a horse ranch."

She met his gaze. "I can't imagine why. I'd have done anything to get out of the city."

The hostility in those whiskey-brown eyes returned. "Is that a confession?"

Angela set her suitcase on the foyer. "You can think whatever you want, Cowboy. The fact is, Reese was about to put his half of this place up as collateral with some high rollers who, trust me, you wouldn't have wanted showing up on your doorstep. I had a pretty decent nest-egg saved, so I offered to buy it outright. He got more than he would've as a bet, and I got a ticket out of the city."

"And how did you happen to be at this 'high rollers' card game?"

She understood the resentment and anger that laced his words. Hell, she still couldn't believe Reese had nearly put up his half of this gorgeous paradise to match a fifty-thousand dollar bet, even if the pot had been worth twenty times that. And big brother may not think so now, but Angela was most definitely the lesser of two evils. She could only imagine the look on his face had Vinnie the Butcher showed up at the door with his goons. "I was the dealer."

He lifted his Stetson and raked his hand through thick, dark brown curls. Angela swallowed the urge to sigh like an infatuated schoolgirl. Reese was a hottie in a dimples and suave charm sort of way, but big brother was easily the best-looking man she'd ever seen. She much preferred his brooding sexuality to Reese's boyish charisma.

"Come on, I'll show you to a guest room." He picked up her suitcase and headed toward the winding staircase that led to the second floor. Angela decided to keep her trap shut about the 'guest room' dig. No sense pressing her luck. At least she was in the door.

She followed him upstairs to the last room on the left. When he swung open the door, she sucked in a breath. The room was stunning—and huge—ten times nicer than anything she'd ever imagined. A king-sized sleigh bed sat against the far wall, the rich burgundy bedding and matching curtains looked like they belonged in a queen's room. The dark oak mirrored dresser, chest, and armchair all appeared to be antique.

He set her suitcase down and glanced around the room, as if lost in memories. "Pretty, ain't it? Belonged to my grandmother. She passed last year."

Before Angela could process that bit of news, he strode to the door and said over his shoulder, "Supper'll be served in about half an hour. If you wanna eat, don't be late."

She winced when the door slammed shut behind him. Okay, so he had reason to be upset—he'd just lost half of his ranch to a stranger. And since he didn't know her from Eve she could let the 'gold-digging opportunist' comment slide, too. But dammit, she was a hard worker, willing to do anything necessary to prove she belonged here. If he'd give her half a chance, she could win him over no problem. She'd worked two and three jobs at a time since she was fifteen years old; no one who knew her would ever accuse her of being lazy. And hell, at least she was here, which was a lot more than could be said about his brother.

Angela did a quick bounce on the bed before hurrying over to look out the window. Miles and miles of lush green hills were dotted with trees and fuchsia wildflowers against a backdrop of the majestic Rocky Mountains and crowned by the bluest skies she'd ever seen. Tears burned her eyes. This was the kind of home she'd always dreamt of having, the kind of home she'd read so many wonderful stories about.

No way in hell would she give it up without a fight.

After trading her pumps for a pair of white tennis shoes, she ran a brush through her hair and headed downstairs, feeling like a little kid on Christmas morning. She was hoping to get a quick look at the horses before supper. Angela had never been on a horse, had never even touched one, but she'd always hoped to learn to ride one day. And thanks to a little thing called kismet, it looked like that day had finally arrived.

That is if James let her anywhere near them.

The house was fairly quiet, although she could hear faint sounds coming from the back. Probably whoever was making supper. She had no idea whether or not they had servants, but she figured they at least had a cook since James didn't exactly look like the chef type, and Reese had mentioned his brother was single.

She slipped out the front door and followed a stone path that led around back. A fenced in area she believed they called a corral was set maybe a hundred feet behind the house, with a structure directly to the left which she assumed was the barn. A lone horse trotted inside the enclosure, and Angela's fingers itched to touch its shiny, chestnut brown coat and matching mane. She hurried over and whistled to the beautiful creature, hoping she could tempt it to come her way. Too bad she hadn't thought to buy a box of sugar cubes. She'd read that horses loved them.

The gorgeous creature turned her way and made a snuffling noise. It tossed its head, and then proceeded to saunter over. Angela clapped her hands, just barely holding in a squeal of delight. The horse stuck its muzzle through the fence, and Angela gently rubbed the bridge of its nose. "Well, aren't you just the prettiest thing I've ever seen. Got a name?"

"His name's Lucky."

Angela swung around in surprise; she hadn't heard James approach. He strode up beside her, propped a boot on the bottom rail, and leaned over to pat Lucky's nose. Again, she couldn't help but notice how attractive the man was. "I suppose there's a story behind his name?"

He shot her a quick look, then returned his attention to Lucky. She figured he meant to ignore her, but after a few moments he said, "I came across him just as a mountain lion had taken him down. If I'd been a minute later, he'd have needed burying, not saving."

Angela gave a delicate shudder. The thought of this beautiful animal being eaten alive was a horrific one. Something she could barely fathom having grown up in the city. "You're a hero then."

His mouth crooked up at that. "Hardly. Just happened to be in the right place at the right time." He stood up and stepped back, gazing past her as if something more important had caught his eye. "Supper's ready. And trust me when I say Meara doesn't like to be kept waiting."

"Is Meara the cook?"

His gaze swung to hers and that coldness she had come to expect returned. "Meara's as close to family as a body can get without being blood related."

"Sor-ry, I was just curious. You know, you really need to do something about that attitude."

"I'll be back to my cheerful ol' self just as soon as you're gone."

Angela made a face at his retreating back. *Good luck with that, Cowboy, 'cause I'm not going anywhere.*

About the Author

USA Today Bestselling author Donna Marie Rogers inherited her love of romance from her mother. Romance novels, soap operas, *Little House on the Prairie*—her mother loved them all. And though it wasn't until years later Donna would come to understand her mother's fascination with Charles Ingalls, Donna's love of the romance genre is every bit as all-consuming. Donna's books have received rave reviews and finaled in numerous contests, including the Aspen Gold, EPIC Awards, and her chapter's own Write Touch Readers Award.

A Chicago native, Donna now lives in beautiful Northeast Wisconsin with her husband and children. She's an avid gardener and home-canner, as well as an admitted reality TV junkie. Her passion to read is only exceeded by her passion to write, so when she's not doing the wife and mother thing, you can usually find her sitting at the computer, creating exciting, memorable characters, fresh new worlds, and always happily-ever-afters.

Website and Blogs:

http://www.DonnaMarieRogers.blogspot.com

http://novelfriends.blogspot.com/